The Chef

Amorous Occupations

I0543431

Cheryl Barton

www.bartonbookpublishing.net

Published by:
Barton Publishing, LLC

This book is a work of fiction. Any references or similarities to actual events, real people, living or dead, or to real places, are intended to give the novel a sense of reality. Any similarities in names, characters, places and incidents is entirely coincidental.

Barton Publishing, LLC
P.O. Box 962
Reisterstown, Maryland 21136
www.bartonbookpublishing.net

Ordering Information:
Quantity sales. Special discounts are available on quantity purchases by corporations, associations, and others. For details, contact the publisher at the address above.

Orders by U.S. trade bookstores and wholesalers.
Please contact information@bartonbookpublishing.net

ISBN: 0615908365
ISBN-13: 978-0615908366

1 CHAPTER

Bang, bang, bang, bang, bang, bang!

Jenna was woke once again. Frustrated of course.

Bang, bang, bang, bang, bang, bang!

There it was again. Whoever was in the apartment above the restaurant next door needed to move the bed to another wall, and not the one connected to her shop. The man or woman obviously had a very active sex life. Jenna only wished it didn't occur so late at night. It's a good thing she didn't live above her bakery, but only used it as a storage area and a place to catch some sleep whenever she worked late, which was the case tonight. Though the noise was an annoyance, it was also intriguing. She could only imagine the pleasure that was being dished out if the constant sound of the headboard continually banging against the wall was any signal. Whoever it was, had been going at it for almost an hour.

Jenna tried catching some sleep, but it continued to elude her due to the activities in the building next door. She was busy working in her bakery for most of the evening and well into the night to prepare for the re-grand opening. Her staff had been sent home hours before she had even decided to give things a rest. All of the preparation work had been completed on the decorating and enough baked items had been prepared to feed an army. Time had gotten away so Jenna decided it would be best to just sleep in her upstairs room so that she could start fresh very early in the morning.

Sleep alluded her due to the amorous activities of her neighbor that was playing havoc, not just with her sleep, but with her mind and body as well. It was a constant reminder that it had been quite a long time since she'd had amorous activities of her own going on and she was jealous. She needed to get up and turn on some music or perhaps the small television she kept for those nights when she did spend the night. Something was needed to drown out the sounds coming through the walls. Since it was so quiet, especially with it being three in the morning, she could hear everything. She heard the wails of a woman who was being thoroughly satisfied. The sounds were making her feel a little tingly herself.

'It's definitely been too long,' she said to herself.

This was her third night in a row of staying over above her shop and it was also the third night in a row that the shenanigans were going on next door. Someone's sex life was on overdrive and it frustrated her more that she couldn't say the same for herself.

When she'd finally had enough, she got up and banged on the adjourning wall hoping it would let her neighbor know that someone could hear them and hope that they would tone it down some. It took a few minutes for her to realize that wasn't going to work. In fact, the sounds seemed to intensify and get louder. It should have annoyed her even more, but it actually increased her own level of arousal. She went in search of her IPod in hopes that she could block out the sounds of the sex-fest next door and get some sleep before the morning crept up on her.

*****

Charles couldn't breathe. He had been going at it for well over an hour. He wasn't sure where this woman had gotten the energy from, but he loved it. The end result was a lack of oxygen, but leading up to it was well worth almost passing out.

Paula was her name and Charles had met her some years back when he had attended culinary school. They had hooked up a few times then and every now and then when she showed up in

Chicago, they would connect again and the night always ended just as it had tonight; with them both needing CPR. They were currently laid out across his bed in the apartment above his restaurant, breathing heavily following another night of great marathon sex. Paula was insatiable and Charles was more than happy to oblige her every time she came to town. It wasn't too often, but when she did, he always knew how the night would end. No strings attached friendships were what Charles specialized in.

He didn't have time for relationships. He was too busy running his successful, award winning restaurant, *'Watt You Say?'* on the first floor of the building. Tonight he and Paula could barely wait until they had reached the apartment level before removing clothes. They'd left a trail of clothing from the bottom of the steps all the way to the foot of the bed. He remembered a flash of something bright red in the form of a bra as he removed it from her body to reveal her large breasts, barely being able to contain himself from massaging them as they poured out into his large hands. Paula had a way of making the blood in his body boil with a need to engage in a night of acrobatic sex, which was the norm for them. She had a body that left a trail of tongues wagging whenever she was in the room.

"Charles, that was incredible, as usual. I look forward to trips that bring me back this way."

"I look forward to every one of your trips too," he replied.

"Well this one will have to tie you over for a while. I'm heading out of the country on business and I'll be away for a few months, but I promise to stop through here when I return," Paula said as she leaned over and planted a hot, wet, opened mouth kiss across his chest, stirring him once again.

"Well, maybe we should do something that will leave us both with an impression of what's to come when you return again," Charles said as he turned, rolling Paula under him again. Seeing her luscious body, he couldn't deny his body what it craved as it once again rose to the occasion, anxious for another round. He knew it was on the moment Paula's long legs went up and curved around his back drawing him down on her.

*****

At what seemed as only a few minutes since he'd closed his eyes an alarm was going off somewhere close by that woke Charles out of a deep sleep. Reaching for the sound that was disturbing him, he realized Paula was no longer in bed with him. He got up to re-orient himself with what was going on when she flew back into the room, quickly throwing on clothes as if she were running a marathon.

"Whoa, what's the rush?" Charles inquired.

"Oh, sorry. I didn't mean to wake you. I forgot

to turn the alarm off. I told you I had an early flight. I called a cab which should be here in a few minutes to take me to the airport. I'm heading back to California before taking a flight abroad for work."

Charles watched her as she flew from one area of the room to the other gathering up the rest of her things.

"Right, you did say that," he said, finally getting up to grab his jeans and some shoes to walk her out. "So, it will be a while before I see you again, right?"

"Yes, but I'll have something good for you when I return," she said, purring a little like a kitten.

Charles was about to comment when he heard the beep of a car horn outside, signaling her cab had shown up.

"Whew. I have to jet."

They both made a dash for the steps. Charles grabbed her suitcase while she grabbed the smaller items. As they reached the door, he snatched up a jacket from behind the bar.

After placing her suitcase in the hands of the driver, they said their goodbyes, looking forward to seeing each other again for more of what this visit was. Charles headed back to the restaurant door, catching a glimpse of movement in the window of the bakery next door. He wondered if it was the person who had banged on the wall the night before, probably pissed at the loud noises coming from his side of the wall. He didn't see who it was. He knew that the previous owner of the bakery had passed away, leaving it to his daughter who was having a two day celebration to re-open the shop. That was probably the reason for her late hours, if it was her, and her early morning waking, to prepare. He would make sure to stop over and introduce himself and get another look at the inside of the shop.

He'd had plans to purchase that building in order to expand his restaurant to accommodate the large number of patrons his restaurant was now experiencing. His recent wins for best Restaurant & Bar Design Award as well as for Best Chef in the Great Lakes area had tripled reservations.

As things were now, reservations had to be made at least a month in advance just in order to get a table. He was sorry to hear of the passing of the owner of the bakery next door and he had been in talks to purchase the building when he was told the owner's daughter had plans to continue with operating the bakery and had no plans to sell. He wasn't a charmer for nothing. He'd find a way to convince the new owner that the bakery would be better in a different location. He'd even take the time to find the perfect spot for it. He just needed to convince her to move; and he would.

Coming in from the cold, Charles made his way through the restaurant, back to the level upstairs to grab a quick shower before heading to his condo a few blocks away. He had a meeting with his lawyer and his accountant before heading back to the restaurant to prepare for the late lunch and early evening crowd. Tonight would be another packed house since they were completely booked. He gave his staff permission to take a few walk-ins if a table became vacant and he always kept his VIP seating area free for when his friends or celebrities came in who wanted privacy while dining.

As he approached the room, the disarray showed the kind of night he'd had. The wild sex he'd had with Paula had them all over the room from the floor, to the dresser, up against the wall, where he could still see his own handprint when he braced himself while Paula bounced recklessly up and down on him. He would remember to tell his cleaning lady to wipe that wall down. He quickly picked up a few things lying around and headed for the shower. It was going to be a long day.

*****

Jenna heard the couple next door as they made their way down the stairs in the building next door and couldn't help herself when she went to the window to get a glimpse of who had kept her up most of the night. Even now she was yawning from not getting much sleep because of their voracious activities. She was already up and working feverishly in the bakery when she heard the cab pull up outside. She looked out of the bay window just in time to see a woman in very high heeled shoes and long flowing blond hair get into a cab after planting a friendly kiss on the lips of the finest man she'd ever seen. Wow, was her first thought upon seeing him. He was well over six feet tall, with lean, muscular legs that she could see via the imprint of the jeans he wore. His skin was chocolate brown with hair black as the night which was trimmed, leading down his face to a goatee that was very neatly trimmed. His face was beyond handsome if that were possible. He definitely had model features. She was so enraptured by his sexiness that she didn't get a chance to move away from the window before he caught her watching them. Even though he had already seen her, she quickly stepped back from the window and tried to slow the rapid beat of her heart.

Looking at him, she had no doubt that her thought from the night before that a woman was getting a workout was indeed what had happened. He looked like his name could be sex. It had to be a sin to be that good looking. If there were such a thing as instant attraction, she had just experienced it and it wasn't due to the fact that she had not been with a man in quite some time. It was because he was deliciously and scandalously fine. What's more? He was right next door and apparently dished out hours upon hours of hot, sweaty, headboard banging sex. She'd heard it for herself and if it had not been for the shower she took to cool her overheated body, she herself would have shot off like a rocket just from listening.

'I really need to get a man,' Jenna said to no one in particular. She went back to getting her shop ready for the opening that would take place in just a few hours.

The ringing of the shop phone startled her considering it was just after six in the morning. Seeing the number, she smiled knowing that a call should have been expected, even in the early morning hour from her aunt.

"Aunt Kat!" Jenna said with lots of enthusiasm. "Good morning."

"Good morning sweetheart. How are things coming along?"

"They are going great. I have a few more things to do, but I'm ready for the opening. Are you still coming?" she asked hoping that the answer would be yes.

"I wouldn't miss it Jenna. I'm so proud of you. Your father would be so proud of you," her aunt said, making Jenna quickly think back to the time when her father was alive. She really missed him.

"I know he would be Aunt Kat."

"I'm glad you decided to keep the bakery open and not close it. Your father spent a lot of years building that business. Even years ago when you'd won the Miss Chicago beauty contest and he wanted to travel with you around to all of your appearances, he made sure the bakery was up and running every day in his absence. I'll never forget the day you graduated from college. It was the one and only time he'd closed for the entire week so that he could celebrate with you."

Jenna remembered that. She herself was shocked when her father had decided to close the bakery for the week to come to her college graduation. He had been so proud of her. For years it had been just the two of them after losing her mother to cancer when she was a junior in high school. It was a time when girls needed their mothers the most and her father had made sure she didn't miss a beat. He made sure she went to every dance, every prom, never missed a dance recital or any of her theatrical performances since she'd loved acting from childhood. She had gone to college to study business so that one day she could start her own business, which would be an after school program for children with one parent or for those who were parentless. It had been her dream until her father had taken ill and she'd spent the last year taking care of him until he'd finally passed away.

"I remember that. I really miss dad, especially today. I'm glad I decided to not sell the business and the building. This is his legacy and I wouldn't have it any other way. I learned so much about cooking and baking from dad. It was because of him that I decided to go back to school to become a Master Baker in order to run this place," Jenna said proudly.

"I always knew you would do whatever you set

your mind to do, including taking over the daily operation of the bakery. I can't wait to see the remodeling you've done."

"It all looks great. It didn't take as much as I thought it would. A new coat of paint was definitely needed and tables and chairs to brighten up the place really helped. I also added an extra oven because I'm expecting lots of additional business especially being next door to the restaurant that won all of those awards the past year."

"Oh right. I forgot about the restaurant. Your father had taken ill just as the restaurant opened and we had to close it when he got too sick to run it. Have you met the owner yet?" her aunt asked.

Jenna thought back to her view of him outside.

"No, I haven't met him yet, but I may have seen him a few times. I've been so busy getting this place back up and running that I haven't had time to introduce myself. I'll be sure and do that sometime today."

"Well I won't keep you. I knew you would be up and I wanted to be the first to congratulate you. I'll see you in a few hours."

"Okay Auntie. I love you. I'll see you in a little while and thanks for the phone call."

Jenna hung up a little sad that her dad was gone, but excited because his vision would continue on. She was also hoping to get the bakery up and running and doing well before she moved on to her other vision of opening up the after school center.

That was next on her list. For now, she had an opening to prepare for.

The three people she hired to work in the shop in the morning and afternoon hours would be arriving soon and her official re-opening would begin. She was excited. Windy City Bakery is about to be back in business once again.

2 CHAPTER

"Mr. Watts. Mr. Cheverly will see you now," the receptionist said, eyeing Charles with a look that he was used to seeing from the opposite sex. When she made a point of sticking her tongue out to lick her lips when she knew he was looking at her, he knew what she had in mind. If only he had the time, but he didn't.

"Thank you," he replied, getting up to head into the conference room to meet with his attorneys. He made a point to look back at the receptionist to give her a wink letting her know he'd get back to her. He continued on into the conference room.

"Charles," his attorney Carl Cheverly said, greeting him. He was also greeted by another attorney, Max who would be joining them for the meeting.

"Carl, Max," Charles said acknowledging them both. "Good to see you again."

"Have a seat Charles. Let's talk about where we

are with the expansion."

"Okay, let me bring you up to date first," Charles said. "As you know, the owner of the building next door to the restaurant didn't sell, but is in fact having a re-grand opening of the bakery later today. I haven't met her yet. The restaurant has been extremely busy and I could never tell when the owner was next door or not. I knocked a few times and each time I got the guys who were doing the redesign of the inside. I may have caught a glimpse of her earlier this morning.

I plan to stop over to introduce myself, but I don't think it's a good time to bring up my desire to purchase her space just yet since she's just doing the opening, but I need to get a plan in place. I need that space Carl. Even though I'm on the end of the block, the only area to expand into would be the parking lot and with the increase in business, I need every parking space. The only direction I'm able to go in would be on the side of the bakery. With all the publicity and awards, reservations are coming in quicker and even earlier than a month early. Business is booming and I'd like to keep it that way. I don't want to keep turning people away because I don't have the space."

"Charles. I understand," Carl added. "Have you thought about moving your restaurant?"

"I can't. I thought about it and I'm in a prime location. I mean, I couldn't have chosen a more perfect spot. The bakery, on the other hand, could actually flourish just about anywhere," Charles added.

It was Max's chance to add in his recommendation.

"Charles. I think the only chance you have of getting that property is to convince the owner that she would benefit from a much more lucrative location, away from other restaurants, especially one like yours that already serves exquisite desserts. She probably won't be able to get much business from your customers. Not many people shop for desserts on a full stomach or they'd buy them at dinner," Max said.

"You are right about that," Charles agreed.

"You could always use your animalistic charm and charm it right out of her. I'm figuring a few weeks of the Watts love and affection and she'd probably give you anything you wanted," Carl added in with a smile, though Charles knew if he'd agreed, Carl would say he was serious about that comment. Charles already knew he was serious, but he wouldn't be venturing in that direction. That's not the kind of guy he is.

"Look guys. Let's all think on how to approach this and make it happen. I don't want anything underhanded done and no Carl, I'll not secure the building by getting in the owners panties."

Carl didn't comment further. He just agreed along with Max to think on the situation and they would reconvene in a week or so.

Charles felt good about the prospects of acquiring the building next door as he left his attorney's office and headed back to his restaurant. He would think on a strategy and get back together with his attorneys to see what the best plan of action would be. He needed that property.

He pulled up to the restaurant and parked in his spot in the back. He headed through the back door and was happy to see his staff hustling about preparing for the evening crowd.

"How are things looking?" Charles asked his restaurant manager, Sean.

"Everything is on schedule. We got that big delivery today and I'm still cataloging everything. I'll leave the final list in your office. Everything has been prepped for you in the kitchen. You also had several messages from friends needing tables tonight. I took two reservations from VIPs for tonight and I'll make sure the usual complimentary items are included."

Charles was more than impressed. He knew from day one when he hired Sean as his restaurant manager, he'd made the right decision. He was always on point and Charles needed and appreciated that. Sean could use a little help in the mighty mouth department though. He knew Sean liked to gossip and he'd had to reprimand him a few times for that. He chalked it up to immaturity. He also hoped that working in this professional atmosphere would also help mature him.

"Sounds like a good plan Sean. I'll check the messages when I get back, but let's go ahead and make the room for my friends who need tables, and I'll call them back when I return," he said.

"You're heading out again?" Sean inquired.

"Yeah, but I'm not going far. I'm going next door to introduce myself to the new owner and pick up a few baked goods to support. I shouldn't be long."

"Charles?"

"Yeah?" he responded.

"She's hot!" Sean said, adding extra emphasis on the word hot.

"Who's hot?" he queried.

"The lady who owns the place next door. She is fine,"

Charles was intrigued.

"Is she now? So you've been over there already?"

"Yes. I stopped over when I got in today. The place was crowded and they even had media. Apparently, she's some type of superstar. Her name is Jenna and she was once Miss Chicago. I heard people talking about it and the media was asking her about the year she reigned. I'm telling you, prepare yourself. She is fine, man. Not just her body either, though the sight of that had me drooling. She is the full package. I'll let you see for yourself. Let me know what you think when you get back."

Charles noticed the smile Sean sported as he

walked away. He figured she must be some looker. Now he really wanted to go next door and check her out along with her shop.

*****

Jenna was more than pleased by the turn out for the first day of the re-opening of the bakery. She wasn't sure what type of reception she would get after the shop had been closed for so long. After her father had taken ill, she didn't have a choice, but to close it up.

Her father had been so hands on with everything that she knew she wouldn't be able to handle it along with taking care of him. Friends and family suggested she place him first in a nursing home and then in hospice when he had gotten worse, but she wouldn't her of it. To focus on him, she needed to put the bakery on the back burner.

Initially when he first died, she had planned to sell it and put it in the past. It wasn't until weeks later when she'd thought long and hard about it that she decided to hang on to it. She had received several offers from others who were interested in purchasing the building and in the beginning, she was considering it. She knew her father would want the bakery to continue so she contacted the attorney her father had been dealing with and worked to get the bakery up and running again.

Today's showing of so many people proved she

had made the correct decision. Not only had customers shown up, but media had come as well. People still remembered her as Miss Chicago and were shocked to see her now running her father's bakery.

She was thanking the latest group of customers who had shown up to support by making many purchases when she looked up to see the man she'd seen in the wee hours of the morning outside of the restaurant next door. Her heart stopped, realizing he was just as handsome as she thought he was. From a distance he was fine. Up close and personal now, he had a rough, rugged kind of sexiness happening. He was built like a god and his handsome facial features would make any woman take a second and a third look at him, even if she was with another man. He was just that good-looking.

Jenna felt nervous as her neighbor headed in her direction. His gaze never left hers as he maneuvered through the crowd, coming her way.

"Hello, my name is Charles Watts. I own the restaurant next door," he said extending his hand out to her.

"Hello. I'm Jenna Taylor. Proprietor of this shop. Nice to finally meet you. I was planning to stop over to introduce myself, but preparations for the opening consumed all of my time," she said, almost forgetting to breathe in between words.

Jenna couldn't figure out why he made her so

nervous. She did realize that she was holding the hand of the man who was giving a woman the time of her life the past few nights on the other side of her wall. The images, a little more vivid than she'd like them to be at the moment, swamped her and her palm became a little sweaty. Even wiping them off on her apron didn't help much. She suddenly felt heated watching her neighbor as he looked around the shop.

"You've done a great job with the place here. I hadn't been here long before it closed, but I do remember a little bit about the inside. You've done lots of upgrades."

"Yes. My dad was running the place back then and had plans to update things around here, but he never got around to it."

He turned and looked at her again before he spoke.

"I was sorry to hear of your father's passing."

"Thank you. I remember the beautiful floral arrangement from the businesses on the block and I remember seeing the name of your restaurant on the card, so thank you for that."

"I didn't know your father well, but I hear he was a great man."

"Thank you and thank you for coming to the opening."

"No thanks needed," he said, looking around at the crowd. "I hear you even had the media out today. This is a pretty big deal for you huh?"

Charles asked.

"They're here more for who I used to be than for who I am today, but that's okay. I'll take the publicity for the bakery, even from nosey reporters."

"Right. My restaurant manager, Sean, told me we have a celebrity next door. Miss Chicago, I believe is what he said?" Charles watched her blush a little. He also realized Sean was right. She was fine. He figured her height to be around five-eight or so and with him being over six-feet tall, he definitely towered over her, which he loved about women, especially ones that interested him. *Was he interested?* Charles thought to himself.

"Yes he's right. That was many years ago. I guess people still want to know what I'm up to since I graduated college, especially now that I'm back in town.

"Congratulations on that. I didn't know. I'm not from Chicago. I landed here after college when I got a gig as an apprentice, fell in love with the city and never left."

Jenna was hanging on every word coming out of his incredible mouth, through the sexiest lips she'd ever been this close to. Seeing him briefly earlier in the morning through the blinds had not done him justice.

"Well I hear you cook up some incredible meals in your restaurant and with the wait list I hear you have to get on just to get a reservation, the city of

Chicago is happy to have you."

She looked up at him with eyes that made him think of being out on a river in a canoe in the dark of night. Her eyes were luscious pools of darkness and he was finding himself being drawn in beyond his control. They were briefly interrupted by a customer who wanted to congratulate her on her opening and to say how wonderful her red velvet cupcakes were.

Charles took in his fill while he had the chance. Though she was wearing an apron with the store signage on it, he could tell she was hiding a scrumptious body. He guessed her cupcakes weren't the only tasty treat. He also wondered how she managed to look comfortable in such high shoes. Having a skirt on, he was able to check out her legs and they were slim, sexy and had the kind of look that made a man imagine how they would look wrapped around his neck.

Charles almost missed when she once again brought her focus back to him. Luckily he was quick and brought his eyes back up her body and on to her beautiful face before she noticed him ogling her like some animal in heat. He didn't want to monopolize her time, but he did want to see her again.

"I'm sorry about the interruption," Jenna said. She didn't want him to think she wasn't interested in standing around talking to him. She was definitely interested in learning more about her handsome neighbor.

"Don't worry about it. This is your opening after all and everyone wants a little of your time. Maybe after things die down, you'll let me treat you to one of those incredible meals at my restaurant that you've heard so much about," he offered, hoping he would get a yes.

Jenna was imagining rockets going off, balloons being released and all sorts of celebratory actions going on in her head when he'd asked, what she believed, was her out on a date. Her mind was screaming, yes, yes yes, but she hadn't yet actually verbalized the words so that he could hear them. She calmed her nerves before replying, not wanting to seem like some love sick groupie or anything.

"That would be great. I'd be honored."

Jenna reveled in his smile of approval at her answer.

"Well I'm going to let you get back to your many guests while I make a few purchases and get out of your way. He pulled his business card out of his pocket and gave it to her. Call whenever you are ready for that dinner. I'm looking forward to it. It was a pleasure meeting you Jenna."

She extended her hand out to his. "The pleasure is mutual Charles," she said.

She watched as he then turned toward the counter to check out the selection. She pretended to not notice him as she continued making her way around the shop thanking everyone for coming in and hearing all of the compliments on the wide selection offered at her bakery. She kept one eye on the walking treat as he made his purchase and headed for the door. Jenna was glad, when before he walked out, he sought her out in the crowd and waved.

"She got to you didn't she? All that fineness got all up under your skin didn't it?" Sean said as Charles walked back into his restaurant with a big smile and his arms loaded with sweet treats from the bakery next door.

"Shut up Sean. Don't you have some tasks that need to be completed," he said jokingly, knowing Sean was correct. That beautiful woman from next door had gotten to him and he hoped she'd call soon about the dinner. He wanted to know much more about her.

"Yeah, yeah," Sean said. "You trying to get rid of me only means I've gotten my answer. I hear she's single too."

Charles immediately thought, here Sean goes again, flapping that mouth of his.

Sean went in for the kill.

"I'm thinking about asking her out."

You would think, from the look Charles was giving him, that Sean had just committed a crime.

"No you won't. Don't even think about it," Charles said, making Sean feel like he needed to back up.

"Whoa boss," Sean said grinning widely. "A little

protective already are we?" he asked with humor in his voice.

Charles continued walking off toward the kitchen.

"Don't push me Sean," he said through the big grin on his face.

"It's a good thing I have a girlfriend or I'd give you some competition with Ms. Jenna," Sean added.

Charles turned to look back at him before pushing open the door to the kitchen.

"Don't kid yourself, Sean. You never had a chance once she met me," he said, laughing loud and hard enough that it made the rest of the staff wonder what they were talking about and what had Charles in such a good mood.

Sean laughed at his boss. "The power of a beautiful woman will bring brothers to war every time," he said finally going off to finish making sure the restaurant was ready for the dinner rush.

Charles didn't want to admit just how right Sean was. The woman next door was on his mind heavily for the rest of the day. While he had been working on special dishes for some friends who were coming in for dinner, he was also planning out the special dinner he would cook for her. He was excited about the possibility of sitting across the table from her and finding out everything.

She was beyond just beautiful. She was intelligent and sweet and no doubt, had a kind spirit. He had also realized, not once did he even think about trying to get her building for his expansion. Somewhere in all of the vivid thoughts he was having about her, he had forgotten about his purpose of going over to meet her, which was to feel her out about the shop. He was losing it. Never had a woman gotten to him so quickly that he was so easily distracted from his purpose. Maybe once he sat down with her, he'd discover she wasn't all that great and that would make things easier for him to come up with a plan.

3 CHAPTER

Jenna was still on his mind later in the evening as he approached the dining area and headed over to greet his best friend, Brad who had reserved a table earlier in the day.

"Brad," Charles said as Brad stood when he arrived.

"Hey man. What's going on tonight, besides this crazy crowd in here? Does the restaurant ever have a slow night?" Brad asked.

"Never man. That's why I'm opening up another restaurant in Vegas soon. People are coming from all over to eat here. I'm hoping to provide them with at least one more option for right now with ideas to expand to other cities around the country over the next several years."

Charles took a seat since Brad's other guest had not arrived yet.

"Is Cecily joining you for dinner tonight?" he inquired, making reference to Brad's fiancé.

"Yes. We are having a night free of any discussions about the wedding. This wedding is turning her into a bridezilla. She's getting crazy with all the planning. I figured she needed a break from any wedding talk or planning. She's taking a cab here from work at the hospital. She wasn't sure how long she'd be. I offered to wait to pick her up and she said she'd just meet me here."

Charles was happy for his friend. He didn't hesitate to say yes when Brad had asked him to be the best man at his wedding. He even remembered the day Brad had introduced him to Cecily. One evening, when Brad called to say he was stopping by Charles' house because he wanted him to meet the woman he had fallen in love with, Charles was shocked to discover that his best friend, who was blond and blue eyed, had walked into his house with a fine sister on his arm. He knew that Brad had dated African American women before, but never thought that his blue blooded family would be happy about his choice for a wife. Charles was happy when Brad informed him that his family loved Cecily. Charles had grown to love her like a sister himself. She was perfect for Brad. He had even offered to host Cecily's bridal shower at the restaurant. He knew that Cecily loved the food and she also mentioned she wanted to show off to her friends that she personally knew Master Chef Charles Watts. He smiled at that revelation.

"You don't have much longer now and all this planning will be over," Charles said, reassuring his friend.

"You're right. Five more months and the love of my life will officially be Mrs. Brad Prescott. I'm more than ready too. She's what I've been waiting for."

"I hear that. Let me know if there is anything else I can do. Cecily is meeting next week with one of the restaurant's event planners to discuss the plans for her shower. I told her to go all out with whatever she wants and it's on me," Charles said.

"You know I appreciate that. This wedding is going down in history as one of the most expensive ever," his friend said, smiling the whole time.

"What's new with you Charles? Who's the latest fling? You know it's time to hang up your player boots and find a relationship or something a little more stable."

Charles brushed that comment off. He liked his boots just fine under the bed of some of the loveliest women in Chicago."

"Don't worry about my boots. They are happy campers. Paula did come in a few days ago. You know how it is when she gets into town. Never a dull moment."

Charles leaned in closer. "I'm surprised I'm even walking today. That woman always puts something on me that could put any normal man in a coma, but you know me. I'm always ready for the adventure and she always brings her best game," he said, making reference to the all-nighter they shared the night before.

"Yeah, yeah. You know you can find that and more in any one woman too. You just don't take the time to get to know them outside of the bedroom to really find out," Brad said.

Charles knew his friend was right, but for now, things worked for him just fine.

"I know you've met a few nice women so why not just invest the time in one and see where things could lead?"

Charles thoughts immediately turned to Jenna from earlier in the day. He could see himself getting to know her if his initial assessment of her was correct.

"I have met some. In fact I met an incredible woman this morning."

Charles watched as Brad perked up, liking the sound of that. Brad always told him he wanted nothing, but happiness for his friend. He wanted Charles to experience the kind of love he was sharing with Cecily.

"Tell me about her. We still have some time before Cecily gets here. She just texted saying she'd just left the hospital which gives us about twenty minutes."

"This won't take twenty minutes. I just met her this morning and I don't really know a lot about her other than she's beautiful and seems really nice and after a few minutes of talking to her, my first thought wasn't about getting her in bed, even though that would be a plus. It was to learn more about her."

"Wow," Brad chimed in.

"Wow is right. Oh I forgot to tell you. She owns the bakery next door."

"Hold up. You mean the bakery that's in the building you're trying to acquire?"

"Yes, that very bakery. I thought I was in a great position to get it when the original owner closed it up because he was ill. His daughter, Jenna Taylor, who now owns it decided to open it back up. I met her today and liked her."

"Uh oh. Something tells me it was a little more than just like, Charles."

"Don't start. I said I liked her. That's all. I did invite her to dinner one night so we'll see if she calls."

"What about the building though?" Brad asked as Sean came over to the table to get Charles to sign some receipts.

"Hey Sean," Brad said.

"Mr. Prescott. It's always good to see you sir."

Charles continued his conversation while signing receipts.

"I don't know about the building. I met with Carl this morning and he had some plan about me getting close enough to her, if you know what I mean, and working my charm on her to convince her that her bakery would be better off in a different location. We even discussed some of those locations. If anyone could make that happen,

34

that would be me," he said, handing the signed receipts back to Sean.

When Sean had left, he added, "but you know that's not me. I don't treat women like that. I don't connive to get what I want, especially not at the expense of hurting anyone, especially a woman. I have a mother and sisters and I wouldn't want them treated that way. I quickly straightened Carl out and told him to look into possibilities that I could share with Jenna and if she says no, then we'll have to let it go. I do have the other restaurant opening in Vegas I need to focus on. A lot of my business comes from out of towners, so giving them another option would help."

Brad agreed. He knew his friend wouldn't purposely set out to deceive anyone and was glad that Charles had set his lawyer straight. Brad's attention wavered when he noticed Cecily. When his smile brightened and Charles looked at where Brad's eyes were directed, he saw Cecily entering the restaurant and heading in their direction. They both stood to greet her as she gave Charles a hug first before planting a kiss on Brad that let everyone in the place know that he was hers. When it didn't appear the kiss would stop, Charles interrupted them.

"You do know this is a restaurant and not a hotel right?"

"Sorry Charles," Cecily said. "I just love this man so much and I've missed him all day."

"Just keep it down some. This is a family restaurant," he said jokingly, that made them all laugh. "I've planned a special meal just for you two tonight so sit back and relax. I'll have a bottle of wine brought right out to you along with some honey walnut shrimp appetizers that I know you'll both love. I'll check back with you later," he said heading back to his kitchen and signally the waiter to bring them a bottle of wine from his special collection.

*****

It had been almost a week and Charles hadn't received a phone call from Jenna. He also hadn't seen her because the restaurant had been so busy. He was also dealing with lots of phone calls regarding his plan to open up a second location of his restaurant in Las Vegas. Perhaps she had been just as busy. He decided to give her a call at the bakery.

"Hello, may I speak with Ms. Taylor, please?" he said when one of the employees answered.

"Ms. Taylor is on another call. Can I have her give you a call back?"

"Sure. My name is Charles Watts, the owner of the restaurant next door. Just let her know that I called please."

"I will. Thank you."

He was in his office hoping she'd call back when Sean called to let him know that Jenna had entered the restaurant looking for him. He could sense the big smile Sean was probably sporting on the other end of the phone.

"Send her back to my office."

Charles was excited. Even more than he would have been with a return phone call. She'd actually paid him a visit. He stood at his office door when she arrived. He finally got a chance to see her without her apron on and she was stunning. She was once again dressed in some very high heeled shoes, something Charles began to assume was just a norm for her. There was something about women's legs in high heels that Charles loved. She had on a skirt and top that hugged her in just the right places.

"Jenna. It's nice to see you. Come in and have a seat," he said gesturing to her to sit on the sofa he had in his office. He sat opposite of her in one of the smaller chairs.

"Thank you. I like your office," Jenna said looking around, checking it out.

Charles nodded his thanks.

"I'm glad you're here. You look lovely," he said, taking note of how she crossed her legs. He hoped he didn't look like some crazy fool, not being able to take his eyes off of her smoother than silk legs. She was so ladylike and he was turned on.

'Keep calm, she's not here for that', he said to his body in his head when it started to react to the sexiness that was Ms. Taylor.

"I'm sorry for not calling you, though I said I would. I was told you'd called me and I figured rather than call you back, I'd stop over, hoping you'd give me a tour of the restaurant. I had some free time and I hope I'm not intruding on your time."

"Not at all. Come on and let me give you a tour of everything."

"This is a grand restaurant Charles. Everything is so elegant and top shelf," Jenna had said at the end of the tour. "I see why the wait list to get in this place is so long. In between the great food, the impeccable service and the ambience of the place, it's understandable."

"Thank you. I'd still like to have you over here for dinner one evening. Why don't you pick a night that you'd like and join me for dinner?" he asked.

"I'd like that. How about you pick an evening when I wouldn't be taking you away from your busy crowd and I'll make myself available," she said.

Charles thought for a minute.

"How about tomorrow night then. Seven in the evening is good for me. What about you?" he asked, hoping she'd agree.

"I can do that. Tomorrow night it is. I need to get back to the bakery. I'll see you tomorrow and thank you for the tour. I look forward to tomorrow night," she said exiting the restaurant.

"So do I," he said at her back when she had left. "So do I."

The dinner was more than Jenna could have asked for. Not only was the food delicious, but Charles had even had a harpist playing throughout the dinner hour, adding to the already romantic tone for the evening. She knew that Charles was well known for creating special meals for friends that no one would be able to find on the menu. Tonight he had done that for her.

Prior to dinner, he had asked her questions about her favorite types of food and if she was allergic to anything. She told him she liked any kind of fish and she especially liked lamb. She wasn't allergic to anything so she looked forward to the surprise meal he would be providing. She had no idea it would be so good.

They had feasted on avocado seafood appetizers, made in a way only found at his restaurant. For the main meal Charles had prepared pan seared lamb chops with rosemary and garlic with an edible leafy garnish that when eaten with the lamb made you feel like a party was going on in your mouth. He had also roasted potatoes in his own special sauce recipe that he said he'd never share with anyone. That recipe for sauce had garnered him several awards. For dessert, she had decided to provide something for the meal they were sharing so she brought with her a molten lava, double rich chocolate iced cake. She could create her own concoctions too. Considering how he dug into the cake over and over, she knew he definitely enjoyed it.

Over the meal they had learned a lot about each other. She shared with him the year she spent as the reigning Miss Chicago and all of the community service she was able to take part in. Something she never did with people she didn't know well, she even shared with him her dreams about opening up a community center one day because it has always been on her heart to do something to help children who were not as blessed as she was with a fantastic upbringing and the support she had from her family. Not every child coming up had that and she wanted to bridge that gap. She talked about what it felt like to lose her mother, especially during the years when she needed her the most, but how her father never let her wallow in pity, but kept her very active.

Charles had shared with her information about his family that lived in Seattle. His parents and two younger sisters still lived there and he traveled home for a visit at least four times a year. He went more often if he found the extra time. His best friend was a guy named Brad who Charles was convinced in another life was a black guy. That made her laugh. She enjoyed his sense of humor. She liked that he was a humble guy who cherished his family and was just as interested in helping build up communities as she was.

"I hope you're having a great time having dinner with me. What did you think of the meal?" Charles asked interrupting her thoughts.

"I'm having a wonderful time. I'm just surprised you actually had an evening where you can sit in your own restaurant to have dinner and not be bothered by guests or your staff."

"I gave them all explicit instructions to not disturb me, but to handle things as they did on nights when I wasn't around. As for the restaurant guests, many enjoy fine dining and have visited enough restaurants where if you see the owner or chef enjoying a meal, it's not polite to disturb them so I don't really have that problem here. Some people recognize me, others just know the name of the restaurant and have gone on the great reviews in order to give it a try."

"That's a great way to operate," she responded.

"I have also enjoyed your company tonight and I'm hoping this won't be the only time I'll get to see you. Maybe we could do dinner and maybe a play or something soon. I like you and I'd like to see you again. What do you think about that?" Charles asked, hopeful.

"I think that sounds like a wonderful idea. I would like that very much. I think I'm going to make my exit so that I can check on the store before I head home."

"Let me walk you out," Charles said, standing to escort her to the door.

"Sean, I'll be back in a few minutes. Feel free to use my table for anyone coming in without a reservation," he said before walking Jenna out.

They stood outside right where the wall separated the two buildings, neither not really wanting to leave.

Charles just liked being in her presence and decided to ask her about her bakery to prolong the time he could spend with her and to also see where her mind was regarding the building.

"You know, before you took over your father's bakery, I had planned to put in an offer to buy the building so that I could expand my restaurant."

Jenna remembered her attorney telling her something about that.

"I'd heard about that. You along with a few others had expressed interest in obtaining the property. I decided it was best to continue with my father's legacy. He had been in this location a lot of years."

"Yes. He was here when I moved it right around the time when I think he'd taken ill. So do you plan to just keep the business small as he did or do you have your own plans for growing the bakery even bigger?"

"I'm not sure yet. My accountant did tell me that the time was right for expansion to increase my revenue. I've actually thought about it a little, but I haven't had much time to really check into things."

That was his in.

"Perhaps I can help with that. Not just because I'd like to purchase your building, but your accountant is right. Due to where you are located, between two other businesses, your options are extremely limited where you are, but if you are thinking of bigger and better, there are a lot of areas that would benefit you better."

Charles watched the play of emotions on her face. He didn't want her to think that he was trying to force her out.

"Listen, as much as I'd like to have your building, I would never offer you any advice just for my own gain. Have your attorney look into it and if you want, I have some people I'd like to recommend who could actually help you with that. Just let me know, okay?"

"That sounds like a good idea. I'll let you know. Well I'm going to head in. Thanks again for a great time and even better food. Everything was delicious," she said.

Charles leaned closer to her before saying, "Especially that chocolate dessert you brought over. I can still taste it on my tongue," he said with a hint of sex added to his tone.

Jenna shuddered at the way he said tongue. Images flashed in her head of the many things she knew he could probably do with that tongue besides eat food. Definitely time to leave, she said to herself.

"I'll give you a call about dinner soon. There is a great play coming to town starting next week that will be here for several weeks. Maybe we can check it out one evening when our schedules will permit it," Charles said.

"I love plays so I'm interested in that. I look forward to hearing from you," Jenna said before walking over to her door and going inside, making sure to give him one last look before shutting the door.

"What a woman," Charles said out loud to no one, but himself. He needed to make a few calls to get tickets to the play. He'd heard it was already pretty much sold out. He also knew he'd have no trouble getting seats.

4 CHAPTER

Jenna couldn't decide what to wear to the play she and Charles were going to see. She had changed from one evening gown to another over and over, having a hard time deciding on which. She decided to text some pictures to Stacey, her best friend who lived on the west coast to see what she would recommend. Before she could send the last picture, Stacey was on the phone.

"Girl, where are you going where you need to be so dressed up?"

"I'm going to a play with a friend."

"A friend Jenna? What kind of friend? A brother type friend or a friend where you need to be sure you have on your sexiest panties, kind of friend?"

"Don't start Stacey. No, not the brother type of friend. He's someone I like and we're going out tonight and I need something to wear. He invited me to a play and out to dinner and I really want to look nice, so tell me what do you think about the pictures I sent to you in a text of each gown?" Jenna pleaded, running out of time.

"I think you should go with the royal blue. Any shade of blue looks good on you and that dress shows off your entire figure because it's so form fitting. Also, wear your hear up."

Jenna grabbed the royal blue one off the bed, placing her phone in speaker mode so that she could continue to talk to Stacey while she got dressed. Now that she had another opinion, when she looked at herself in the mirror, she realized Stacey was right. The royal blue gown was definitely the one.

"Okay, I'm going with the royal blue. You're right, it's the right one for the night."

"Good, now find the right shoes and don't forget the condoms," Stacey yelled in the phone.

Jenna stood stunned at her friend's idea of a joke.

"Stop playing around Stacey. I don't need to pack any condoms. Besides, I don't have any. I haven't been with anyone in ages. If I did find one anywhere around here, it would be far beyond the expiration date. Besides, it's just a date to the play and dinner. We are nowhere near a sex date. At least not yet," Jenna said. "I've only known him about a month."

"Well keep hope alive my sister. It's time to get rid of the cob webs and get you a good old fashion screw."

"Thanks, but no thanks Stacey. I'm good for now, though every time I'm around him parts of my anatomy end up doing all kinds of flip flops. This man is twenty shades of sexy. He is the walking example of sex."

"See what I'm saying girl? Go ahead and get you some. Get you a little or a lot. Jump him if you have to. I'm telling you, it's not normal for anyone to go as long as you have without just a little somethin', somethin'."

Jenna had to laugh at her crass friend. Leave it to Stacey to turn every conversation about any kind of date into a sexfest.

"Give it a rest Stacey. I'll leave that up to you who seems to have no problem tap, tap, tapping everything with three legs!" Jenna said, making fun of her friend.

"Yeah well don't hate. At least I'm getting' some and on the regular."

"Yeah, yeah," Jenna said. "I'm hanging up now. I'll call you over the weekend."

"Bye girl and remember condoms."

"Bye Stacey," Jenna said ignoring her mention of condoms.

She had just finished dressing and donning her last bit of make-up when her doorbell rang. Charles was right on time.

When she opened the door, they both looked at each other as if they were aliens from another planet. It was as if they were seeing each other for the very first time.

"My goodness, you are lovely Jenna," Charles said through glassy eyes. His heart skipped a beat at how gorgeous she looked in a royal blue gown, definitely made just for her. He was able to get a better look at her curves and she had it going on.

"Just when I'm dressed in my best, you come prepared in a dress that's going to make me have to get dirty beating guys off with a stick who'll be looking at you. Maybe you should try a gray sack. I'm sure you'd still look good, but not so good that I'm thinking I don't want to share you with anyone tonight."

Jenna blushed. She had never received such a compliment before, not even when she was Miss Chicago. Back then she received comments from men who clearly hadn't had any home training on how to speak to a lady.

"Why thank you for that. I'd have to say the same thing about you. That tuxedo is wearing you tonight. You look fabulous. Good enough to eat."

Too late she thought. It was already out of her mouth.

The way they were both looking at each other, they needed to leave before they ended up naked on her living room floor.

"Are you ready?" Charles asked, breaking into the heated moment and changing the direction of thoughts that were running through both of their heads.

"Yes I am. Just let me grab my bag."

When they were comfortably seated in the limousine Charles had rented for the evening, Jenna was able to sit back and relax and take in the evening. She had been looking forward to the night ever since Charles had called her confirming he was able to get tickets. He let her know that he hoped it was okay that she could be meeting his best friend and his best friend's fiancé tonight. Brad was able to get them seats together in a box that was center stage. Jenna was fine with meeting his friends. She hoped that meant that he was liking her as much as she was him since he had no problems introducing her to his friends. Over the past month, they had talked several times on the phone and he had come over to the bakery to talk and share in a cupcake or two.

They pulled up to the theater amidst lots of glitz and glamour. The best of the best in Chicago, including some major entertainers were in attendance and Jenna loved the electricity that was in the air.

She watched as Charles prepared to exit the limo only to turn back around before doing so.

"I've needed to do this since I picked you up, so I hope it's okay with you," he said to her.

Jenna wasn't sure what he was talking about until he leaned in close to her right before planting a sweet soft kiss on her lips. She gladly accepted it.

"Thank you. Now we can go," Charles said right

before getting out to come around to the other door to help her out.

*****

The play had been superb. Charles and Jenna were now having dinner at a local restaurant with Brad and Cecily having a great time.

He especially liked how well Cecily and Jenna were getting along. They had connected as if they were long lost friends. At the end of the night, he liked that they had made plans to do lunch or coffee one day. He was really beginning to like Jenna a lot and the fact that she fit in well with his friends was a bonus.

They were now back in the limousine headed back to her place. The silence in the car only added to the sexual tension that was clearly in the air. Charles had noticed the way Jenna had been looking at him the whole night. He had been looking at her the same way. He was trying to be as gentlemanly as he possibly could but being in such close quarters with her in that knock out gown that gave him that come and get me message all night long, he wasn't sure how much longer he'd be able to hold out.

Any minute now, he would have to end up sitting on his hands to keep from reaching out for her. They should probably engage in some small chit chat just to pass the time by until they reached her house so that they could refocus the sexual energy they were both exerting into something a lot less tempting.

"What did you think of the play," Charles asked her.

Jenna's mind was far from being on the play. All she could think about was, where was a condom when you needed one? For once, she wished she had listened to Stacey because she was so aroused, she couldn't imagine letting him go home tonight without a little taste. She'd tried to stay engaged in the conversation with his friends and she really did like them, especially Cecily, but as hard as she tried to take part, she couldn't help imagining Charles' hands all over her body and hers all over his drawing pleasure out for hours on end. All that thinking and here she was in the back of a limousine with him and he wanted to talk about the play.

She would play along if that's where his interest was.

She turned towards him giving him her full attention.

"I loved it. I don't go to enough plays. I have been known to donate to various causes of the arts, but I haven't had the chance to actually sit and enjoy them like I did tonight. Thank you for inviting me."

The ride continued like that all the way to her house. They talked about everything except the fact that they wanted to rip each other's clothes off.

When they pulled up to her door, Charles got out to again come around to help her out. When they arrived at her front door, Charles didn't want to leave. He wanted to come inside and not just inside of her house. He wanted inside of her.

After Jenna found her key, she turned around to face him, giving him a chance to see the want in her eyes and hoping he would take the cue. She has never been the type of woman to take the lead with a man, but if he didn't soon make a move or at least offer a suggestion to put them both out of their misery, she would take a page from Stacey's book and go for it.

"Thank you again for a wonderful night Charles."

Charles was done.

"Invite me in Jenna," he said in an alluring manner.

Jenna wasn't expecting that. She was expecting a little more banter back and forth. This is what she'd wished for and the ball was now in her court.

"I thought you'd never ask," she said opening the door for them to enter.

"Jenna," Charles said with a husky sound to his voice.

She turned.

"Do I need to ask the driver to wait for me?"

Jenna's stomach quivered at the way Charles' eyes seemed to darken when he asked that question. Oh yeah, she thought. She wanted this.

She didn't even hesitate.

"No, you don't."

Charles' eyes never left hers as he reached for his cellphone and told the driver to have a nice night. As he closed his phone and placed it back in his suit jacket pocket, they both heard the limousine as it pulled away.

Not being able to wait another moment, Charles pulled Jenna to him and without hesitation, he took her mouth with a fierceness that seemed to suck the breath right out of her. His mouth claimed hers over and over as she returned the kiss with hunger, to claim ownership of his mouth as well. They dueled like that until the passion began overtaking them both. Before either could register what was happening, Charles had pressed Jenna up against the nearest wall, letting her feel how hard and ready he was for her.

"We need a bed," Jenna said between kisses that continued to plunder her mouth.

"If it's not in this room we're in now, it'll be too far away. I need to get in you right now," he said, breathless.

Jenna couldn't agree more.

Without much effort, she reached to unzip his pants as he reached up under her gown to pull down what appeared to be the skimpiest thong he'd ever seen in his life. When he finally removed it, he placed it in his jacket pocket at the same time that he withdrew a condom from his back pocket.

Jenna was excited when she realized he had thought to have one handy. She had never had sex without a condom before and she shuddered to think that she would have considered being careless without one because that's how much she's wanted him inside of her. She's glad one of them had a level head.

While he tore at the condom wrapper to get it open, Jenna slipped her hand inside of his pants and stroked his hard as steel flesh, eliciting something that sounded like an animal sound out of him. Feeling him grow even harder and thicker under her touch brought her great pleasure. She loved that she was able to do this to him.

As he donned the condom, he saw a sofa that would do in place of a bed. He wanted her to be comfortable. He picked her up, unzipping her gown as he walked with her butt cheek in one hand and the other on the zipper of her gown, tugging it down. When he reached the chair, Jenna released her legs that were wrapped around his waist and the gown slid to the floor. She hadn't been wearing a bra so she stood before him only in very high heeled royal blue stilettos that matched her dress. When she leaned down to remove them he said, "Leave them on. I like the shoes and skin look you have going on.

Jenna smiled deviously. She felt even more sexy.

She helped him to quickly remove his clothes

and before she could get a good look at him, he had lain her back on the sofa, joined her and immediately joined their bodies. They began moving together as if they were doing a dance choreographed perfectly just for them. The room began spinning. It didn't take Jenna long to become undone. The way he was making her feel could no way prolong the inevitable. Her orgasm crashed over her and she held on tight to Charles as he endured his own release. Clearly this was something they both desperately needed.

They never did make it to the bed. What they had done was work up an appetite. After Jenna put on Charles' dress shirt, which came down far below her knees, he slipped on his dress pants while she went in search of something to quench a new thirst they both had; one for food.

Jenna returned with sandwich wraps, fruit, cheeses and a bottle of wine. They made themselves comfortable in her living room while they dined.

While she had been in her kitchen, Charles had noticed papers sitting on her table and he could easily see they were a proposal that he himself had put together. Jenna must have taken the information he had suggested to her about the possibilities available to her if her bakery were in another location, and contacted the guy he recommended to her. He hoped she looked over the information carefully. It was a lot to consider.

Even though his original idea was to give her the information and they both could benefit, his focus had changed. He still agreed that a move would be a good one for her. He also knew that with his help, she could also acquire more business in her current location. All it would take would be a recommendation from him to other restaurants in the area that contracted out the business of desserts and her business could triple. He felt like a heel knowing that his initial desire was to acquire her building. Now he didn't care about that at all. What he did care about was her. He was beginning to care about her a great deal.

He watched as she set all of the items out so that they could relax and enjoy.

"So, while you were in the kitchen, I noticed you have the papers about the other property for your bakery. What did you think?" Charles asked.

"I see where it can certainly be beneficial. I'll have to take more time and think it over. I'm not so sure it's for me," she replied.

"Well like I said, if you need any help from me, let me know. I'm available."

5 CHAPTER

Weeks had gone by and Charles and Jenna had settled in to a nice routine. Due to how busy their schedules were, they found that the best time for them to spend time together when they couldn't take an entire day was late at night. That worked for them both. They often found themselves working late in their respective businesses so some nights, Jenna stayed with him above the restaurant and others, he stayed with her above hers. The best times were when they could squeeze a full day and night out at the same time and it was during those times that they stayed far away from the restaurant and the bakery and spent time at each other's houses.

Tonight appeared to be one of those nights where they both were working late. It was pretty late at night and he could hear music coming from the bakery. Her staff never stayed this late, so Charles knew it had to be Jenna. He decided to lock up and see if she was okay before he headed home.

He called the bakery line, hoping it was her that picked up.

"Charles, hi," Jenna said with great excitement in her voice.

"Hey yourself. I was leaving out of the restaurant when I noticed the lights were still on in the bakery. Is everything okay?" he queried.

"Yes. I'm just trying a few new recipes for some new cupcakes and time got away from me. I was just going to bake until I got tired."

"It's not safe being in there alone this time of night and leaving out."

"I know, but I parked my car in the garage that's connected to my building so I feel pretty safe when I leave out at night."

"Would you like some company for a little while?"

"Sure. Are you sure you're not too tired? I know the restaurant was crazy busy tonight."

"I would never be too tired to spend time with you."

"In that case, I'm coming out from the kitchen to let you in right now."

"Okay," Charles said hanging up his phone, waiting at the door for her to open it. When she did, his arousal for her went to a whole new level. She was wearing stretch yoga pants and a tank top with only socks on her feet. Even dressed down she looked sexy and he liked it a lot. He watched as she mixed batter. Watching her work and the sway of her lovely hips to the music was intoxicating. She was so focused and his mind went to all the things they could be doing with the creamy mixture in the bowls. Charles decided to test his theory.

He came up behind Jenna, reaching into the bowl of cupcake mix. He placed a little on the tip of his finger before putting the finger in his mouth to taste it. It was the most erotic action Jenna had ever witnessed, watching that one finger the whole time, even after it had disappeared into his mouth. She couldn't speak. The moment didn't call for any words from her at all.

"This is delicious," he said removing his finger from his mouth, making sure he licked every drop of mix from it first.

They stood with their eyes transfixed on each other as he reached into the bowl for another swipe with his finger and this time he brought the finger to her lips for her to taste.

Jenna's heart was racing. She was already about to become undone. Without thinking she slowly opened her mouth, allowing Charles to insert that one finger coated with batter to enter. Once his finger was in her mouth, she closed her lips around it and proceeded to lick all of the sweet, creamy batter from it while he moved his finger around in her mouth making sure she tasted every drop. He removed his finger sooner than she thought and before she could speak, he did so first.

"Isn't that the best tasting batter you've ever had before?" he asked her, knowing it was a crazy question to ask a Master Baker, but the moment called for a little teasing.

"Better than you can imagine," Jenna replied, still not taking her eyes from his. She continued looking over her shoulder at him as he took that same finger, placed it in his own mouth and mimicked what he had just done with it in her mouth.

"I have to agree with you. My finger has never tasted better," he said, seductively.

Jenna couldn't do anything, but swallow.

"You do know that I'll have to throw out this batch of batter now. Not saying your fingers are dirty, but you know how it is."

"How many cupcakes would that bowl of batter make, Jenna?" he asked, turning her fully around to face him.

"Thirty-six with this batch."

"Good, I'll write you a check for them because I have some private plans for more of the batter and I wouldn't want you to lose any money from what I'm thinking of using it for," he said dipping his finger once more in the mixture and swiping it across her lips.

Before she could get her tongue out to lap it up, Charles leaned in, capturing her lips and the batter at the same time. As the kiss continued, Charles reached in again into the batter, drawing some of the creamy mixture up with two fingers this time and wiped his fingers across her neck. When he proceeded to lick and kiss the batter from her neck, Jenna knew she needed them both naked before she took her next breath.

Charles sensed what she was thinking. He wanted her as much as he could tell she wanted him, but he wanted to have a little fun with her first.

"Shall we take this to the room above your bakery, Jenna?" he asked softly while still kissing around her neck.

"Yes."

"Great and we won't have to worry about being quiet because no one is in the restaurant at this hour," he said happily.

"Yes, the walls are quite thin," Jenna added, not forgetting the night before they had met and what he could hear through them.

"Right," he said, still licking her neck. "I remember now. You like banging on walls. That was you wasn't it?" he asked, feeling her body stiffen when he did so.

When she didn't answer, he tried to first relax her again and then coax her into responding by soother her with caresses on her arms. He wanted her to feel comfortable sharing anything with him.

"We could stand here all night and I could continue to find places to put more batter where I see exposed skin, but this would be a lot more fun if we were in a room with a bed. You have to answer me first though."

"It was you wasn't it? You heard me that night before we met and you banged on the wall because of the, let's just say the noise was bothering you, keeping you awake perhaps?" he inquired further.

Jenna nodded her head.

"Don't nod Jenna. Say it baby."

Hearing him call her baby sent juices that were making her panties soaking wet.

"Yes. I heard you. I could hear you and a woman."

"Were the sounds turning you on? As turned on as you are right now," he continued whispering against her skin, causing goose pimples to rise and making her nipples as hard as pebbles, painfully straining against the front of her bra.

"Wouldn't you agree that a night with me is much better than hearing it through thin walls?" he asked teasing her even more by sliding his hand down the inside front of her pants and into her panties to swipe his finger across her other set of lips.

Jenna almost shot off on the spot. Her body was already more stimulated than it had ever been and any touch could be *the* touch.

She watched through heavy, hooded eyelids as Charles removed his hand and placed the same finger back in his mouth, tasting her essence as he had done with the batter.

"Now this cream is better than the cream in that bowl behind you," he said making sure she watched him lick her cream from his finger until it was all gone.

Jenna was ready. She didn't want to be teased anymore.

"Charles, don't make me beg," she said, almost pleading.

"As much as I'd love to take you right here on this table in your kitchen, I'm sure the board of health would have a different idea of how non-hygienic that would be. Do you have any reservations about me taking you upstairs right now?"

Jenna was already grabbing his hand and heading towards the steps before he could get his next word out.

"Wait Jenna," he said.

She was now getting very frustrated with how he was prolonging giving her what she needed.

"Charles wait for what? I don't want to wait anymore," she said impatiently while taking his hand once again and heading towards the steps.

"Wait. Let me grab the rest of the batter," he said, just as impatient as she was. "You can't bake with it now anyway and I'm imagining quite a few uses for it."

Jenna could imagine that as well and like him, she wanted to act on it. Not waiting for him, she went back to the table, grabbed the bowl, pushed buttons on the wall to activate the alarm and hit a switch that turned off the lights in the shop. She would clean up the kitchen in the morning before her staff arrived.

Charles picked her up, careful not to spill any of the batter and carried her up the stairs, skipping steps while hurrying to get her naked.

Once they reached the landing, he went in the direction of the room with the bed.

Jenna's body tingled at the thought of what was about to occur. She'd had some steamy dreams about him on the nights that they weren't together and she knew the reality was much better than any dream she could possibly have.

Rather than place Jenna on the bed, Charles slid her down his body so that their bodies still touched. He took the bowl of batter from her and place it on a side table next to the bed before coming back to her and without words, his eyes went straight to her mouth and Jenna knew exactly what he wanted. She wanted the same thing.

She leaned up as he leaned down and the fusion of their mouths was electrifying. Jenna opened up to Charles as he plundered her mouth with his, drinking his fill like a man who had been lost in the dessert and her mouth was the only fountain around.

She became as desperate for him as he was for her.

Charles' assault on her mouth was relentless and Jenna matched him in her own assault on his lips. They only came up for air when they needed to breathe. Her hands desperate roamed up and down his back as she felt his all over her body where it seemed like he had more than just two hands. Her entire body was on fire from his touch and his kisses.

Jenna had never been so thoroughly kissed before and she wanted it to last forever. She moaned against his mouth when she felt him finally attempting to remove some of her clothing. She willingly lifted her arms above her head so that he could remove her tank top. When her arms were free again, she reached to tug his shirt out of his pants in hopes of getting her hands on more of his skin. She wanted to put her hands all across the muscular chest that she had been thinking about since he'd entered her bakery tonight.

Charles helped Jenna get his shirt off and he didn't waste any time after it was gone in removing the rest of her clothing that was keeping him from seeing her in all of her delicious glory. He'd grown to love seeing her naked. Her body was meant to be without clothes on it. He reached for the waistband of her pants and pulled them along with her panties all the way down her legs and off to the floor. Before long, the rest of his clothing except his boxer briefs had joined her clothing. She stood before him in only a bra and socks and she admired the body that showed proof of how good one could look when they worked out often. Clearly Charles did, she thought.

Jenna didn't hesitate to lean in and lick from one side of his chest to the other driving him a little more insane on each passage. The moans that she thought may have been coming from her mouth were actually emitting from in between his lips and if she thought she couldn't get any more aroused, she did.

Charles needed to slow things down. He didn't want to rush to the finish line with Jenna. He wanted things slow so that he could savor every moment. He quickly took a step back to get a good look at her. She was magnificent in his eyes. He couldn't help but stare at her perfectly contained breasts and was afraid he would go crazy if he didn't soon remove them from the bra that confined them.

"Turn around for me Jenna."

Jenna didn't hesitate to comply. When she did, she felt him reach for the clasp of her bra removing the lacy material and when it dropped in front of her, he reached around and cupped her mounds, rolling the nipples between his fingers. She was in heaven. His hands felt perfect. She had more than a handful, even for his large hands and he was slowly caressing and kneading them, letting her know how much he enjoyed them.

"I love your breasts. I could spend the entire

night just focused on them and I'd be satisfied. Perhaps though another night. Tonight, I don't want to leave any part of your body untouched by me."

As he continued his ministrations, she could feel his arousal as it pressed hard, long and very thick against her back. She was anxious for him to remove the last piece of clothing that divided him from her, but he was having none of that when she reached around behind her to try and pull them down.

"No sweetheart. Not yet. If I let you do that, this is going to be over fast. It's already taking every bit of strength to hold off as long as I have. You definitely bring out the beast in me and for a few moments, let that animal stay confined until I've made you purr," he said, rolling the 'r' between his lips, dragging it out.

She could barely take it. The teasing was driving her wild with want and insatiable with need.

"Charles I need you. I need release so bad. Do you want me to beg?" she asked as she laid her head back on his chest while his hands continued roaming over her over-sensitized body and down further toward the apex of her thighs. He was heading right where she needed him and when he reached his goal, she slowly opened her legs, widening her stance more to give him easy access to that part of her that was screaming for his touch.

Charles slid his hands between her legs and

discovered she was indeed still dripping wet for him. He knew she needed him and he didn't make her wait long at all. With them still standing with her back up against his hard, straining erection, he slid first one, then two fingers inside of her where fluid drenched his fingers, running down them like a faucet.

Jenna moaned and began grinding against the fingers that sought entry into her and when they had found it and Charles began using his thumb to stroke and caress her knotted nub, Jenna couldn't help, but fly to higher heights as an orgasm took over her body. She tried to suppress the scream that was released from her mouth, but couldn't. The force was too great and she couldn't contain it. While she rode the crest of the wave after wave of pleasure that was consuming her, Charles didn't let up. He used his other hand to tweak and pull on her nipple just the way she liked which drew her orgasm out even longer.

Just when she was about to collapsed, Charles' arm reached out to steady her even while two fingers still worked inside of her body.

Charles licked around her ear and said, "Now that's what I needed the most. I wanted to feel you lose control and come apart in my arms. Now let's see how adding a little batter to the mix can help take this to the next level."

Jenna could barely move or hardly see. Her mind was still jumbled from the orgasm where she was still seeing stars behind her eyelids.

Before she could register what was happening, Charles had lifted her up into his arms and placed her on the bed while he reached for the bowl of batter.

Jenna was in a haze and only knew that more pleasure was in store for her. She only hoped she could survive the onslaught. It would not be a good look to pass out from pleasure in the middle of a night with a gorgeous hunk of a man.

Even through her haze, she could make out the impression of his engorged member through this briefs that were barely containing him. He was so long and thick that the briefs no longer covered his manhood completely. She could see the head and over half of him sticking out of the top and pressed against his stomach as if it was taking a peek out and waving at her. Her mouth watered at the thought of getting her lips wrapped around it or as much as she could. She would never be able to take the full length, but she wanted to give it her best effort.

Her fascination with his penis was short lived when Charles returned to the bed with batter covering his hand.

"I hope you have other sheets because I think these will soon be completely covered in batter and juices."

Jenna didn't have time to reply. Before she could, Charles had reached out and made a path on her body from her breasts to the dark, thin line of hair covering her womanhood. He waited no time at all following that same path with his tongue.

She was trying to breathe through it all, but the feeling was overpowering. She was lost, consumed by the primitive need to just lose all control. When his tongue had finally reached her core, she didn't know what to do. She tried to focus on being in the moment with him, but her body wanted to go to a higher plane. It wanted to go where there was pleasure and nothing else. She could feel Charles all over her body and not just near the entrance to her body. She stiffened wanting to hold on to the orgasm that was coming in order to draw out the pleasure. She didn't want to release it too soon. He was making her feel so good.

"Open for me baby," Charles said when he saw her straining to control her body's reaction to him.

Jenna gave him what he wanted. She spread her legs wide open for him. When she did, he reached up to push the back of her legs further toward her chest so that he could settle in for, what seemed like a feast. At least it looked that way from her viewpoint. She gave herself over to him freely knowing what the end result would be.

Charles watched as Jenna's body jerked on the first pass of his tongue along the lips that encased the hard, moist nub that was staring back at him. He knew it wouldn't take much to send her over the edge and when he used his tongue to enter her body, going in and out, then in again and this time while coming out, he pulled and tugged on that nub that he knew would send her over the edge and that's exactly what happened. As he lapped up every bit of her body's essence that flowed into his mouth, Jenna screamed his name over and over. When he could have let up, he didn't. He kept going, plundering into her body with his tongue until he noticed she was almost as limp as a rag doll from pleasure overload.

While Jenna worked to control her breathing, Charles took the time to grab a condom from his pants pocket, removed his briefs and quickly donned it to protect them both.

He leaned down to give her a deep, penetrating kiss, allowing her to taste her own essence on his tongue before asking, "Are you ready for me baby?"

Charles said that while rubbing his flesh up and down the seam in between her legs giving her a hint of what was to come.

Jenna was more than ready. She proved it by grinding up into him so that he briefly slipped into her body.

He was surprised by the move and the excitement of what he felt set off embers in his brain.

He knew she was clearly as ready for him as he was for her. He didn't make them wait any longer.

Charles reached down to gather her legs up so that they rested in the crook of his arm, widening her legs even further so that he could plunge into her body easily. With one long, hard thrust he entered her. He went in and out of her body again and again bringing them both so much joy that the only sounds heard in the room were of his moans, her groans and the sound of flesh slapping against flesh. It wasn't long before Jenna was quaking again. Her orgasm triggered his as they both shattered into a million pieces, screaming each other's names as they rode out their pleasure. Any vestige of control, either had, went out the window as their moans changed into screams of pleasure unlike anything either had ever experienced before.

Something new for Charles was happening. He had just experienced one of the most powerful orgasms he'd ever had and already, he felt his body building up for another one. He was wild with want and that animal that he tried containing all night was now free and loose in the room. While Jenna still rode out the crest of her release, Charles saw rockets just before he erupted through another orgasm, immediately following his first.

He heard himself growl because the feeling was out of this world. The feeling was so great, he realized he was pounding into Jenna and she was loving his wild abandonment. She coaxed him on by meeting him stroke for stroke, rising up to meet his downward thrusts and whispering over and over to him how much she loved what he was doing to her.

Charles and Jenna laid like that, with him still in her body, laying on top of her for what seemed an eternity.

Jenna felt better than she ever had in her life. This man had made her body do things and react in ways that had never occurred before. The intensity of his lovemaking inspired her to lose control like never before. She was laying under him, loving the weight of his body on hers. When he finally released her legs so that they could relax, and he attempted to move to take his weight off of her, she wrapped her legs tightly around his back holding him in place.

"Don't move. I like having you on me like this," she said.

Charles was glad because as much as he probably needed to move, he wasn't sure he had enough strength to do so.

"This was some workout", she said right before Charles leaned up and took her mouth in a searing kiss that gave her promise of more to come.

"I'm glad you feel that way," he said when he could once again find the energy to speak.

They laid that way for a few more minutes when Jenna wasn't sure if he had fallen asleep or not. She tried to look over at him to see if his eyes were closed.

"I'm not sleep," he said. "I don't intend for either of us to sleep tonight."

Jenna smiled knowing he meant every word.

"That's good because I hear sleep is overrated anyway, especially when there's a fine man in bed who's naked and who has the stamina of a stallion," Jenna added.

"Well this stallion has plans for you and the rest of that batter."

As soon as he said that, Jenna felt him hardening once again.

"I see this is going to be some night, but first, it's my turn to get creative with the batter."

Charles was excited to hear that. He rolled off of her body, reached for the bowl and handed it to her.

"Take all the turns you want baby," he said happily, and she did.

*****

"Jenna. Wake up baby."

Charles knew she had to be tired. They hadn't gotten more than an hour's worth of sleep before he realized he needed to get going before her staff showed up, catching them all sticky with cup cake batter. He didn't know what she wanted her staff to know about them, but he was sure it wasn't the scene that was before him at the moment, which was them naked in a bed covered with remnants of a mixture of their sweat and cupcake batter. He tried waking her up again.

"Jenna come on. It's about to be daybreak. What time does your staff come in?" he said, trying to stir her. That got her moving.

"What time is it?" she asked trying to come awake.

"It's five in the morning."

Hearing that, Jenna jumped up.

"Oh my goodness. They'll be in around six. I need to get up and clean up the kitchen, along with this room." She looked around at the mess they'd made. She got excited just remembering all that they had done and the many ways they'd come up with to use the batter. Jenna knew she'd never be able to look at another bowl or another cupcake for that matter and not think of Charles, naked in her bed doing, naughty, unspeakable things to her and her to him. They had spent other nights above the bakery, but he had never been here this late in the morning. They always tried to be sure things were back to normal before either of their staff's showed up in the morning.

"Do they come in this room during the day?" he asked.

"No."

"Then I would say worry about this room later. Just lock the door. I'll get dressed and start cleaning up the kitchen downstairs while you get a shower. I'll shower over at the restaurant. My morning crew will be arriving around seven to begin prepping for the lunch crowd so no need in me going home. Go ahead and hop in the shower," Charles suggested as he began getting dressed.

"Wait, you need to take the alarm code off before you get in the shower so that I can go downstairs."

"It's six, six, two, one, nine," she said before running into the bathroom.

When he found his shoes, he put them on and went down to straighten up the kitchen as much as possible. No need in the staff knowing that something other than baking had taken place the night before.

Jenna was happy at the scene before her when she entered the kitchen.

"Thank you for cleaning all that mess up. They would have thought something had happened to me if any of my staff had come in and seen everything out of place. I never leave the kitchen unclean even after my late night baking."

"Good. It's going on six. I'm going to leave out the back just in case any of them are coming in early," he said walking toward the back of her store.

Charles turned when he reached the door. He pulled her into his arms to steal one last kiss before leaving.

"I'll call you later. Try to get in a nap during the day while your staff is around to help. We got no sleep last night and we don't want to be walking around like zombies. I know I'm going to try before the dinner rush. I'll call and check on you later," he said snatching one last kiss to get him through the day.

"Okay and Charles? I had a wonderful time last

night or rather this morning."

He smiled, liking the sound of that.

"So did I sweetness." On that, he went out the door to get next door to the restaurant to get a quick shower before his own staff showed up.

*****

Jenna spent the day trying not to yawn in customer's faces. She also tried not to blush every time someone asked her about a cupcake. Any thoughts of cupcakes took her back to the night before with Charles and the many ways they had used the cupcake batter. After the first go 'round, she had taken the batter and had spread it all over his body and took her time licking it off. The height of the adventure had been when she'd wrapped her batter covered hand around his erect flesh, stroking him while spreading the batter from tip to base.

After he was breathing hard enough to induce a heart attack, she replaced her hand with her mouth and the reaction she received from him fueled her even more. The part of him that wouldn't fit into her mouth, she used her hands along with her mouth to pleasure him. When he tried to convince her to stop before he lost control with his member in her mouth, she continued her onslaught as he had done to her, until the taste of him filled her mouth. She had never done that before, but with Charles, it was exactly what she'd wanted to do.

The memories kept her going all day, longing for a time when they could be together again. She was sure it wouldn't be today. They both needed rest. They had slept very little and they both had very demanding jobs.

She decided when she could no longer control her yawns, to leave the store in the very capable hands of the manager and two other employees. She went home for the evening in desperate need of sleep and a real good bath. She had taken a quick shower, but she needed to be sure she was able to get all of the cupcake batter off of her body especially from all of the places that Charles had continued smearing it throughout the night and well into the wee hours of the morning.

She hadn't been home long when her phone rang. It was Stacey. Jenna had completely forgot they were supposed to have a conversation about her visiting Stacey soon and they promised to talk tonight. She was tired and wanted to get a bath and into bed as soon as possible, but she missed her friend and wanted to catch her up.

"Stacey!" Jenna screamed happily into the phone.

"Hey girl. What's shakin'?" Stacey asked.

"Not much. I'm about to grab a shower and hit the sack like a ton of bricks."

"Wow, the bakery has you tired like that already? There must be some serious sugar lovers in

Chicago."

Jenna knew it wasn't the customers that had her this wiped out.

"Not really," she said, wondering if she should tell Stacey the truth. They never kept things from each other and Jenna could always tell her everything.

"What is it is then? Spill Jenna. I can hear it in your voice. Something's up."

"Well sort of. It has to do with this cupcake batter I really need to bathe and make sure I've washed it all off," she said through a smile that she knew Stacey would be able to sense through the phone.

"Oh Jenna you are nasty girl. Tell me everything," her friend said excitedly. "This Charles guy sounds like a real trooper; just the person to keep those cobwebs from forming again. Hit me with it."

"Let's just say that in the last twenty-four hours, I've only slept about forty-five minutes."

"Oh it was that good huh?"

"Oh yeah, it was better than that good."

"Damn, I'm jealous. Does this guy have a brother, a cousin or even a father that's single?" Stacey quipped and they both laughed hysterically.

"Well I won't go into too much detail about the night, but I will tell you more about him."

Rather than bathe and get in bed early like she'd planned, she spent the next few hours filling her friend in on what she knew about the Master Chef next door who was completely rocking her world.

*****

The day flew by and Charles didn't get a chance to check in on Jenna. After having his usual morning meeting with his staff, he'd disappeared into his office to grab some sleep before he had to switch into chef mode for the evening. Luckily he had the best kitchen staff around and he wasn't always needed to cook. He did make sure that he checked every dish that would be prepared so that it was up to the standard that his patrons were expecting and were used to.

He hoped that Jenna had gotten some extra sleep in throughout the day. He knew she had left a little earlier. He'd seen her car pull out of the garage in back when he was in his office. He assumed she was heading home, especially if she was as tired as he was, and he was exhausted. He would be leaving soon to head home himself. He wouldn't call her tonight. She needed her rest. He would stop over at the bakery the next day. Spending all night making love to her had taken its toll.

His plan of hitting the bed the second he got home didn't happen the way he planned. His attorney had sent over some papers that looked like he may be getting Jenna's building after all. They had talked several times where she'd asked for his advice and he gave her his honest opinion. He knew that she was planning to visit her best friend in about a week or two and she wanted to have things moving forward while she was gone.

Charles was even surprised at the price Jenna was considering letting her building go for. He knew she could probably get more for it and he would make a note to tell his people to make a larger offer than the low ball price she was asking for when it came time to bid on it. He was falling for her hard and not only did he not want to take advantage of her, he didn't want anyone else doing so either. He made corrections on the documents and faxed them back over so that Carl could have them first thing in the morning.

6 CHAPTER

Jenna was all set for her trip to visit Stacey. They had both decided it had been too long since they had connected in person and they had a lot of catching up to do. It had been a few months since the bakery had reopened and business was doing pretty good and Jenna felt that at least for a few days, she could entrust the bakery into the hands of her staff.

She packed early in the day because tonight, Charles was preparing a special dinner for her at his house. He wanted to spend time with her before her flight out in the morning. She placed her bags by the door so that even if she were late getting back home, everything would be at the door and waiting for her.

As she went about preparing to go to Charles' house, she realized she was humming. She was happier than she ever thought she'd be. Charles was a wonderful man and he was all hers. She not only loved being around him, she was in love with him. There was no doubt of her feelings for him. She only hoped he felt the same way and that they were going in the same direction with the relationship. She loved him and trusted him. She especially trusted his opinion with the advice he gave her about her shop. From the outside looking in, I would appear to others that Charles' advice was purely to gain her building but she didn't see it that way. She saw it as him opening up her mind to the possibilities and helping her achieve them because he cared so much about her. They were committed to each other. She wasn't seeing anyone else, and neither was he.

During one of their late night talks, he'd told her about the woman he had been seeing when they met and assured her that was over. She was all he could handle. That thought made her giggle. She liked that she gave him what he needed and he didn't feel the need to supplement elsewhere.

She had decided to make a move on the new location for her bakery. Financially it was the right move for her. She would miss being right next door to Charles but she was secure in the relationship they had and she didn't need to be next door for that to continue. She would discuss it with Charles, but not tonight. Tonight was about love and spending time together because she was going to miss him while she was away. She was planning to put something on him that would tie him over until she returned. The little sexy, barely there number, she had placed in her overnight bag was just what she needed. She was all set for a night with the man she loved.

*****

Charles had finally finished prepping for the dinner he was planning for Jenna. This trip of hers to the west coast would be hard on him not seeing her for almost a week. At least it wasn't an entire week. He knew she was planning to return in time to attend Cecily's bridal shower that was being hosted at the restaurant. They were actually becoming good friends since the night they'd met at the play. He didn't want to make the night just about sex or making love. He wanted it to be about quality time spent together. They were far beyond just being together for the physical pleasure.

She had somehow seeped into his heart in the months since they'd met. He never thought he'd be in a steady, committed relationship, but here he was. He had even stopped communicating with Paula. One night she had called when he and Jenna were at his place enjoying a movie and he had not hesitated to let her know that he was in a relationship and he couldn't be in contact with her anymore. She had first laughed at him thinking he was joking, but he assured her, with Jenna listening, that he meant every word. He wished her well and ended the call. He hadn't heard from her since and he was just fine with that. Jenna was all the woman he needed.

She had called to say she was just a few minutes away.

As soon as Jenna rang the doorbell, Charles was there to greet her, taking her into his arms for one of those magical kisses she always looked forward to. She loved when he was aggressive with her. She had to constantly remind him that she wouldn't break.

When the kiss finally ended, they were both already out of breath.

"Wow," Jenna said. "I'll take a hello like that anytime."

"You can get it whenever you want it," Charles added. "Come on. Let's get this evening started. It will be time for you to leave sooner than we think. What time is your flight out?" he asked.

"It's not until early afternoon, but I plan to get to the airport early. My bags are already packed and at the door."

"Good because it's my plan to keep you here with me until the very last second," Charles admitted. He was so sprung. He knew it and didn't mind at all.

After the incredible dinner he'd cooked for them, they decided to settle in his living room to check out some movies and just enjoy the closeness for the night. They didn't always need sex to have that and tonight proved that. Being close without being naked was just as fulfilling.

They sat together, cuddling up on his sofa when Charles felt the need to share his feelings with her.

"Jenna," he said, getting her attention.

She didn't look up from her position of lying across his chest. She just acknowledged him, continuing to look at the movie.

"I love you," he stated, without any doubt in his voice. He wanted her to know he meant it.

When she did look up at him, she knew she was feeling exactly what he was feeling.

"I love you too Charles. I have for some time now. You've made me happier than I have ever been. I never thought I'd finally find someone who completes me. I'm thankful it's you."

"Jenna, never in my wildest dreams did I ever think I'd be uttering those words to anyone. With you it seems so natural, so right. I wanted to be sure before you left here to visit your friend that you knew there wasn't just me here waiting for you when you returned, but my love for you would be here waiting too."

He sealed the moment with a kiss that spoke volumes for the love he had for her and Jenna readily received it.

*****

Jenna was running late. There was a last minute

emergency at the bakery so she decided to stop through on her way to the airport. She was glad she'd made sure she wasn't doing everything last minute so she didn't feel rushed. After getting that under control, she decided to stop over at the restaurant to see if Charles was in. Perhaps she could get one last kiss from him before leaving for the airport. The restaurant appeared empty when she entered it, considering it was still pretty early in the day, even for the lunch crowd. She had just come in the door and was heading towards his office when she heard Sean talking to the bartender. She was about to interrupt them when she heard Sean mention her name.

"Man I'm excited about this move to Las Vegas. You guys will be busy here also now that it looks like Charles will finally get his wish and expand the restaurant into the building where Jenna's bakery is," she heard Sean say.

"Right, so that deal went through?" the other guy asked.

"I really don't know, but with how happy Charles has been these days, it has to be because he was able to charm his way into Jenna's heart and convince her to sell her building and I'm sure he'd be the first to make a bid on it."

"What do you mean charm his way? That doesn't sound like him. I think he really likes her Sean?"

"Yeah well. You may or may not be right about

that. I heard him telling Brad that his lawyer had told him to get close to her because that would probably be the only way to get her to even consider it since she didn't want to in the beginning. I actually heard him say that Carl, the attorney guy, told him to use his charm like a pipe piper and once he had her hook, line and sinker, he was in for getting that property. He knew how women can't resist him."

"Is that right," she heard the bartender say.

"Well if that's the case, then I guess that's why Charles has been floating around here on cloud nine. He has been wanting that building since he first opened the restaurant. I guess the power of persuasion stems from the Johnson in his pants." They both laughed.

Jenna was devastated. She was hurt and glued to her spot on the floor. She couldn't believe Charles would do that to her and then to find his staff was standing around laughing and making jokes about it. So it was all a game to him? He said all the right things and did all the right things just to get her building.

She turned to leave, bumping into one of the bar stools, drawing the attention of both men. She looked at them before bolting from the building, jumping in her car and pulling off. As she drove off, she could see Sean in the rearview mirror after he had come out after her. He was now standing at the curb watching her leave.

"Now you've done it Sean," the bartender said, joining him at the curb.

"Charles will be out for blood for this one. I'm telling you, I think he's in love with her and you just ruined it."

Sean knew he was right. He was in a world of trouble.

Charles was in his office, sure he would have heard from Jenna before her plane took off. He would give her a little more time before checking to be sure she had arrived at the airport okay. Every time he thought about her he smiled. He guessed being in love did that to a person. He had wanted to share something else with Jenna the night before, but they had agreed to not talk any business. That was fine with him. He would wait until she returned to tell her the good news. He reached for his phone before the office answering system would pick up.

"Restaurant, *"Watt You Say?"* this is Charles," he said into the line.

"Charles. It's Carl."

"Hey Carl. Tell me you still have good news for me."

"That I do my friend. Everything is looking good. The plans for the community center are being drawn up and should be ready by the time Jenna returns from her trip. We also were able to get the okay from the city regarding the expansion for your building. Since you are located in an area that is non-residential, they are okay with some construction happening over night as not to disrupt too much of your business or the business next door. You just need to go over everything with Jenna and as long as she agrees, everything is a go. You must really love her to be doing all of this for her."

"Yeah Carl. I love her very much. I'm just glad everything is working out. I'm investing a lot of money in this community center and the other investors are just as excited as I am and as I'm sure Jenna will be. This has been a dream of hers," he said while reaching into the top drawer of his desk to retrieve the small box that held his future.

He listened while Carl ran other business matters by him and he took another look at the ring he was planning to put on Jenna's finger the moment she got back in town. He knew before he even told her the night before that he loved her that he wanted to marry her. Knowing she loved him, he was sure it was the right time to propose. He closed the ring box back up and placed it back in his top drawer where it would sit until he came up with how he would propose. He wanted it to be something big and over the top. He had a few days to think about it.

After his call with Carl ended, he got a little more paperwork done before calling to check on Jenna. He was surprised when she didn't pick up. She must be checking in at the airport. He would wait a few minutes before trying her again.

Sean paced nervously outside of Charles' office trying to come up with an easy way to tell him how badly he had screwed things up. No matter how he approached it, his boss would be furious. He sucked it up and knocked. When he heard the usual 'come in', he opened the door and stepped into the lion's den.

"Hey boss."

"Sean, why can't you just call me Charles like everyone else? Is the word boss really necessary?" Charles asked. When Sean didn't respond, he looked up and noticed something very different about his restaurant manager. Something major was bothering him. It wasn't noticeable just on his face, but in the way he paced nervously in front of Charles' desk.

"What is it Sean and how much is it going to cost me?" he asked figuring it must be big.

"More than you think and the cost is not money. I think I may have screwed things up real bad," he said nervously.

Looking back at the papers on his desk, he let Sean explain figuring he must have screwed up an order or something.   Not lifting his head he said, "Screwed what up? Spill it Sean."

"Well, I sort of screwed things up between you and Jenna."

Charles sat straight up when he heard Jenna's name. What could Sean have done that would screw things up with Jenna? he thought.

"What did you do," Charles said with a little more force behind his words.

"She kind of overheard me talking, making a joke that you were playing her to get her building for the restaurant expansion."

Charles knew he had to be hearing things. He stood up violently, knocking over his chair in the process.

"What!" he shouted. "Tell me you're joking Sean."

"Wish I could boss, but I'm not. I'm really sorry. I was talking to the bartender about the expansion. He was wondering if it was going to happen and I sort of told him about the conversation I overheard you and Brad having one night about how your lawyer recommended you charm the building out of Jenna."

Sean became more nervous and borderline scared as Charles came around his desk and stood right in front of Sean looking down at him like any moment he would pounce, especially since he already felt like he was in the lion's den.

"Are you crazy or just stupid Sean? For starters you shouldn't have been telling anyone about anything you overheard me say. Second, that was not the end of the conversation I had with Brad. I also told him that I in no way agreed to do anything like that nor would I ever if it meant hurting anyone. Lastly, you could have just ruined the best relationship with the most wonderful woman in the world," he said, clearly upset.

"I know and I'm sorry. Really I am. I tried to catch her to talk to her and apologize, but she was really upset. Mike, the bartender, noticed her standing there before I did and he said he thinks she was crying when she left."

Charles' mind was reeling.

"When did this happen Sean?" he asked trying to figure out if he had time to catch Jenna before her flight left.

"About an hour ago."

"An hour? What took you so long to come in and let me know?" he asked with more anger than Sean had ever been on the other end of before.

Charles didn't give him a chance to respond. He went back to his desk and immediately dialed Jenna's cell phone.

"Get out Sean. If my relationship is over, so is your job."

"Sorry Charles," Sean said, exiting the office.

No answer from Jenna. After several rings her phone went to voicemail.

"Jenna, it's Charles. Call me baby. I need to talk to you. I know you're probably at the airport by now so if you can, call me before you board. I love you."

He hung up, now completely distracted. Jenna would be gone for almost a week and if he didn't clear this up before she returned, he knew he could kiss the relationship goodbye, all because as usual, Sean couldn't keep his big mouth shut. He knew looking at the time that he'd never make it to the airport in time before her flight took off so he would just keep trying her cell until she answered.

*****

"Stacey. It's Jenna," she said into the phone finally able to reach her friend. She had been excited to have a little time off to visit her best friend whom she missed a lot. She missed being able to share everything that was going on in her life with Stacey over drinks or dinner. It was times like now that she really needed her the most.

"Jenna. Are you about to board," Stacey asked. "I can't wait for you to get here."

When Jenna didn't answer, Stacey became concerned.

"Jenna. Are you still there? Is everything okay?"

"No Stacey. Everything is not okay. He's been using me and I had no clue. I fell in love with him and he's been using me the whole time."

"What are you talking about, Jenna? I don't understand what's going on. Who's been using you? Mr. Wonderful?" she asked.

Jenna smiled at the term Stacey used for Charles from all of the wonderful things she's always sharing about him.

"Yes, Charles."

"Jenna I don't understand. Start from the beginning. Using you how and for what?"

"He faked real interest in me so that he could talk me into selling him my building and relocating my bakery. It was all a scheme."

"I don't believe that Jenna. After everything you've told me about him, I find it hard to believe it was all a ploy just to get your building. He's rich. He can get any other property he wanted. He wouldn't have to do that. I can't see him being that desperate. It's just a building. Why do you think he was using you?"

"I overheard his restaurant manager telling someone about the idea his lawyer gave him to do whatever he could to use his charm to get closer to me," she said, through the strain in her voice, attempting to hold back the cry that wanted to escape. She was devastated.

"I've been such a fool Stacey. This was the first relationship I've ever had that I really thought was genuine and it turns out he is no different than other men who used me as a self-serving opportunity." Following those words, she really did start to cry and Stacey heard it too.

"Jenna, sweetie, are you sure? What did Charles say when you confronted him with what you overheard?"

"Nothing. I haven't talked to him. He's called and left several messages, but I haven't talked to him."

"You have to. You need to. I don't believe that he would do such a thing. Maybe you misunderstood what you heard?"

"I don't think so. I know what I heard."

"Okay. Where are you? Are you still home or at the airport already?"

"I'm at the airport, sitting waiting for them to call my flight."

"Okay. Listen to me. As much as I really miss you and want to see you, I want you to get your things and go back to the restaurant and talk to Charles. You can't just go by what you heard and you certainly can't spend five days out here on the west coast with me with this weighing on you the whole time. If you talk to him and he admits it then you know it's over, but you have to give him a chance to explain himself. You can visit me anytime. For now, handle your business. No more running from things. You have to confront him and do it so that it's all out in the open."

Jenna knew her friend was right. She needed to talk to Charles. She wasn't sure she could do it right now. She was still so angry at him.

"You're right, but I really want to come see you," Jenna said.

"You can still do that. Just get a different flight for later in the week or if need be, I'll fly to Chicago to visit you instead. I haven't been since your dad's funeral anyway and I don't mind taking the trip. I have some free time. Right now though, go work on your relationship. Don't leave it like this. Think about all of the things you've told me you about him. You did say in the beginning when he first mentioned trying to buy your building, you thought it was a little strange, but that as you got to know him, you realized that though he was interested in it, he was giving you good advice on whether you moved or whether you stayed. That doesn't sound like a man who is setting out to set you up. Do you really think he would go to that length? "

Jenna was beginning to realize that Stacey may be correct. If nothing else, she needed to have Charles explain everything to her. She at least deserved some honesty. She had never felt this way about a man before. Could she really have been that naïve?

"You're right as usual. I'll call you tomorrow okay?"

"Okay. Call me if you need to talk anytime. We'll talk tomorrow about new arrangements for a visit."

Jenna disconnected the line, grabbed her bags and exited the airport. It was getting late and Charles would be in the midst of a busy evening at the restaurant. She would go spend the night at the bakery and try to catch him before he went home for the evening. They needed to talk and it needed to happen much sooner rather than a lot later.

7 CHAPTER

Bang, bang, bang, bang!

Jenna almost leaped out of her bed above the bakery. She must have fallen asleep while waiting for the restaurant to close so that she could talk to Charles.

Bang, bang, bang!

There it was again. She had to be dreaming. There was no way she was experiencing déjà vu. Thinking she must have been dreaming, she was about to lay her head back down when it happened for a third time.

Bang, bang, bang, bang!

"No," she quietly said to herself. Jenna sat staring at the wall as her heart sped up at the thought that Charles was with a woman above his restaurant.

"How could he?" she said while holding a hand

over her heart, trying to slow it down.

Her Charles, the man she loved; the man whom she had given her heart to was in his apartment above his restaurant having sex with another woman. Charles was cheating on her. She was, after all, supposed to be out of town tonight.

She guessed his restaurant manager was correct when she overheard him telling another employee how Charles was only using her, getting close to her so that he could talk her into selling her building. She couldn't believe it.

Her first thought was that Charles was a snake and she was angrier than she'd ever been. After taking some time to think about it, she wanted to give Charles a chance to tell her the truth. He had led her to believe that his ideas on other locations that would best benefit her shop were on the up and up. She believed that he truly had the best intentions with his suggestions. She had to admit that the locations he had recommended would benefit her much more because most of the restaurants that surrounded here also served desserts so customers patronizing them would be less apt to patronize her business going in or coming out of those establishments.

She appreciated that Charles had even offered to help her secure contracts with some of the restaurants to sell some of her desserts. That would really be a big business boom for her. She could expand her shop to handle more business contracts, something she couldn't do in her current shop due to space constraints. She had bought into everything he'd told her and was actually considering the move after talking with her accountant and her financial advisor. They thought it would benefit her business plan as well. She had also called one of her cousins, Thomas Atwater, who owned a financial investment company in North Carolina with his wife Karen. They had also taken a look at the business plan for a possible move and thought that it was a good move for her. Even with all of that, it still hurt her that Charles thought he had to be deceitful in order to get what he wanted.

Now she sat alone in her shop listening as Charles made love to another woman as if he had not just declared his love for her the night before. No matter what she knew she had to move now. Even though things were clearly over between she and Charles, she was moving on from the location and from the relationship she thought they were having. It was apparently a relationship that only she was in. He obviously had other ideas for what a relationship was. She was listening to his idea through the wall and it obviously involved a lot of panting and screaming.

As the moans, groans and banging got louder, she couldn't stand it anymore and decided to go into her kitchen to do some baking. She only hoped she could stop crying long enough to not have a new ingredient, tears, as part of her latest batch of cupcakes.

*****

Charles woke up realizing Jenna had never called him. He had finally gotten home after a long day and evening at the restaurant hoping she would have cooled off enough by now to talk to him.

The dinner crowd had kept him busy the entire night. He had also gotten the chance to talk to Brad as he and a few of his buddies had dropped by the restaurant and they'd spent most of the evening talking about how stupidly happy and in love Brad was.

He was excited for his best friend. He was in love with a good woman and Charles was happy when his friend decided to pop the question. He and Cecily were a perfect match; almost as perfect as he and Jenna were. That was until Sean opened his fat mouth and Jenna had overheard him making a comment about how Charles had been using her in order to get his hands on her building.

He really couldn't be too angry at Sean. He had said those words to Brad, but Sean didn't hear the entire conversation. Now that he had calmed down, he wouldn't actually fire Sean. It was clear all evening that Sean was wondering when that ball would drop. He was still apologizing and Charles finally let him off the hook by telling him to forget about it and that he would work it out with Jenna when she returned.

Before he left for the evening to head home, he informed Sean that it was okay to let Nathan close the place up. Nathan was the head waiter. He told him that Nathan would finally be learning the ropes since Sean would be taking over running the Las Vegas restaurant when it opened. Charles knew he was a big screw up, but he trusted him when it came to how he ran the restaurant and was thankful when he'd agreed to take over the new location. When he did so, Charles would promote Nathan to the manager of the Chicago location. Charles had another reason why he was allowing Nathan to close up, but Sean didn't need to know that. He had already proven that he couldn't keep his mouth shut. Charles would work with Sean on that before he took over the new location.

He was just about hope in the shower when his ringing phone startled him. He was so engrossed in his thoughts, he wasn't sure what the sound was. He thought that it may be Jenna so he reached for it quickly and saw that it wasn't her, but that it was Brad.

"Brad," Charles said.

"Hey Charles. I just wanted to say thanks again for hosting Cecily's shower this weekend. I forgot to mention that last night."

"No problem. That's what friends do."

"You're right. One day when dreams of wedding

bells are invading your sleep, I'll return the favor somehow."

Charles chuckled thinking that would be cool if he ever got that far.

"Right. Like that will be happening," he laughed.

"What? All the great things you've told me about Jenna don't tell me it hasn't crossed your mind at all? Man you couldn't meet a more perfect match for you."

Charles couldn't agree more, but the current situation of his relationship with Jenna was still up in the air since he had not heard back from her.

"She is perfect and definitely perfect for me."

"Then what's the problem?"

"I may have indirectly screwed things up," he said with concern in his voice.

"What did you do? I know it wasn't another woman because you are completely sprung on Jenna. What's up?"

"Remember that conversation we had at the restaurant about that idiotic advice my attorney gave me about charming Jenna into selling me her building?"

"Yeah, I do."

"Big mouth Sean let the conversation slip and she overheard it. The thing about it is, he only heard the bad part of what I was telling you. Not the part about how I would never go along with such a thing."

"Oh, wow. Sorry to hear that, man."

"Were you able to at least talk it out with her, after you read Sean the riot of course?"

"Not yet. I've tried calling her. She won't call me back. She was scheduled to visit a friend for a few days so I'm assuming it'll wait until she gets back. I would like to talk to her before then. I don't want this to simmer for an entire week, eating away at her and I can clear this up with a conversation."

"So she went away thinking you've been lying to her and planning some diabolical scheme in order to obtain her building?"

"That's about right Brad. If she would just call me back, I could fix all this."

Charles hesitated before continuing on sharing his true feelings for Jenna.

"I'm in love with her Brad."

"I knew it," Brad shouted into the phone, loud enough that Charles had to move the phone away from his ear.

"Yeah, yeah. Don't say anything else about it."

"I've never heard you say those words about a woman before. Have you told her? Does she know?"

"Yes I've told her, but at this point, I'm sure she doesn't believe me."

"Don't let it go down like this Charles. I'm sure when she's calmed down some and is thinking logically, she'll be able to see that you're being genuine. Maybe a few days is what she needs. She may be too angry to even listen to you right now so let her have a few days."

"You could be right about that," Charles said.

"Plus, you know she's invited to Cecily's shower on Saturday, so if you don't talk to her before then, try to talk to her then. I doubt if she'll make any kind of scene with all of those women around."

"I don't know about that. I don't want to catch her off guard if she's still angry, to try and explain everything the day of the shower. I'll figure something out, but I do agree, she probably needs a few days to think things through. I was so pissed off at first that I was going to fire Sean. That's not the first time he's had a problem keeping his mouth shut. Luckily I know more about his good qualities, especially when it comes to running the restaurant. I also know he meant no harm. He didn't know she was listening."

"Don't be too hard on him Charles. Get your focus off of what he did wrong and try to fix things with Jenna as soon as she gets back," Brad added.

"That I plan to do expeditiously. There is no way I'm letting my relationship end over something so trivial. I've got some plans for Jenna that I'll share with you in a few days. I've been working on some things that I've been planning to do for her and I still hope to do that even if she no longer wants to be in a relationship."

"I'm sure you're over thinking this. Since I heard you say the word love, I'm already planning on what my tuxedo for your wedding is going to look like," Brad said, laughing trying to lighten up the conversation."

"Let's see how this goes first before you start making plans for tuxedos other than the one for your own wedding.   Speaking of, I'll see you tomorrow when we pick up our tuxes for your wedding. Also, thanks for the advice."

"That's what best friends are for. Catch you tomorrow," Brad said before hanging up.

Charles expected that by the end of the weekend, he and Jenna would be back on track or he would at least die trying to make things right.

*****

Going to the gym to get her work-out on was the best idea Jenna had had in a long time. It helped worked out some of the frustration she was currently suffering through. Since she had already planned to be away from the bakery for a few days, she'd left a note for her staff that she had spent the night above the shop and that she had done some baking, in case they were wondering where all of the extra baked goods had come from. She decided to not visit Stacey and would call her later in the day to tell her not to worry.

She had her answer about Charles. He had definitely been playing her because he was back to his old tricks of bedding women above his restaurant. She figured it was probably Paula, the same woman he had been with the morning she'd first laid eyes on him. She knew that the woman had called Charles one evening when she was at his house and he had informed her that he wouldn't be able to see her anymore because he was in a relationship. She guessed that must have been purely for show since she was in the same room with him when his phone rang.

Now she realized since he was expecting her to be gone until Saturday, he had time to play until her return. She hoped it was well worth it to him to play her like he did. She wouldn't be a wounded victim. She was stronger than that. Even though the idea about moving her bakery was a good one, the way Charles went about handling it was underhanded and she would never forgive him for it. She had planned to talk to him, but hearing him through the wall having sex killed any idea she had of listening to anything he had to say. He may be able to explain away what she overheard Sean saying, but there was no story he could tell her to fix what she'd overheard the night before. It was over with him.

She knew Cecily's bridal shower at the restaurant was coming up on Saturday and she still had plans to go. She may have to deal with Charles then, but by then, she would be ready. She was going to take the rest of the week off, ignore his phone calls and enjoy some much needed time.

"Stacey. It's me Jenna. Listen, I'm not going to come out this week. Some things have come up that I need to focus on here, but I will call you and we can reschedule my visit or plan for you to visit me. I decided not to talk to Charles. I got my answer when I overheard him having sex with another woman last night so we didn't, nor will we, have a chance to talk about anything. I will fill you in later on. I'll call you tonight. Love you girl," Jenna said as she disconnected the line. She was glad her friend hadn't answered. She didn't really feel like talking. She needed some time to digest all that had happened and planned on figuring out how to get over Charles.

She still couldn't believe the turn of events and how quickly things can change. Hours ago she was living a fairytale. She was in love with a man who loved her in return. Her business was really taking off and she was looking forward to how her business could grow in the future.

Deep down, she really hoped that there was some type of explanation for all that had happened. There had to be, she thought.

8 CHAPTER

Charles watched as the love of his life entered his restaurant and when she didn't smile when she saw him, he knew that she was probably furious with him. He had to explain. He stopped her before she had a chance to walk into the bridal shower that was being held for Cecily. He knew from her determined steps that she had no plans to stop and talk to him, but he was just as determined.

"Jenna. We need to talk," he said, adding firmness to his voice. He didn't want her going into the shower on fire with anger at him.

Jenna took a step back when he approached, not out of fear, but out of sheer disgust for the images running through her mind of him with another woman in his upstairs apartment.

"We have nothing to talk about Charles and I'm

already late for the shower," she said, speaking just as firm as he had. She didn't want to fall for any more of his charm. It was that charm that got her to the state of embarrassment that she was now experiencing.

"I think we do and the shower can wait Jenna," he said.

Her anger began building even more at his insistence. How dare he, she thought. If he wanted to talk, then fine. Maybe getting her thoughts out would alleviate her going into the shower and everyone being able to tell that something was bothering her. Before he could speak she went in on him, adding attitude to her words by placing her hands on her hips for added measure.

"Talk, you want to talk? Fine then let's talk. Where should we start? Should we start at how you've been making a fool of me for the past few months pretending to be interested in me just to get your hands on my building? You are a snake Charles. All the things I'm remembering you saying to me, was it all a lie? Did it mean that much to you to have my building? That's cold-hearted even for you," she said, making sure to stress each word, lacing them with fury.

"I heard Sean talking about your scheme to get close enough to me to make me fall for you so that you could take my shop right from under me while at the same time taking my clothes, literally off of my body. Should I be appreciative that you are courteous enough to find me that wonderful other spot for my bakery so that you could make it look like you were really only thinking about helping me expand my business? A win, win situation for us both is how you looked at it? She kept her voice as low as she could in case anyone from the shower was nearby. No need for everyone knowing how much of a fool she had been for him.

When Charles could finally get a word in he tried to explain.

"None of that is true and you know it. I meant every word I've said to you. I've been trying to call you for the past few days to explain, but you wouldn't take my calls. I knew you were out of town and I figured you were too angry to talk then so I've been waiting for you to get back. I wasn't sure you'd make it to the bridal shower today. If you will let me explain I know I can clear the misunderstanding up. I do admit, Sean listened in on a conversation I was having with Brad one evening in the restaurant, but he didn't hear the entire conversation. My attorney did make a sly comment about using my charm to talk you out of your clothes and out of your building, but he was only joking. I knew he was joking, but I set him straight. I let him know it wasn't like that and I'd had no plans of ever doing that. Every minute spent with you was on the up and up. I was with you because I really wanted to be, not to get your building. That's the truth Jenna."

He reached out to pull her to him and she again, stepped back from him, but he continued on.

"I didn't make love to you for any underhanded reason. I didn't fall in love with you for any personal gain. I did so because you are an incredible woman and any man would be happy and very lucky to have you in his life. I have felt that way from the beginning and it hasn't changed. When I told you I loved you, I meant it and I still do. I love you Jenna. Don't do this to us. Don't cheapen what we have by believing I would do this to you; to us."

When Charles thought she would soften on the words he spoke from the heart, it appeared, they only fueled her anger more.

"Me cheapen? Really Charles? You think I'm cheapening what we had?"

He didn't miss that she said the word 'had', as if they were over.

"I got your calls and I listened to your messages and I didn't believe any of it. I knew from the beginning you were interested in my building. All the advice and help you were offering me about other locations because it would help me appear to be a much bigger brand by increasing the size and being able to put out more product with a larger kitchen and being able to produce more by hiring more staff as well. When I first heard it, I thought it was a good idea as well. What I didn't realize was you weren't doing it for me, you were doing it for you. I guess the incredible sex was your icing on the cake, I presume? That's what I call cheap Charles. That you would do that just to get my building for your own expansion. Well you can take it and shove it. I wouldn't want to continue being next door to you every day, disgusted at myself for how I allowed you to take advantage of me."

Charles was angry at himself. He never wanted to hurt her and even though he tried to explain how untrue her thinking was, he could see how she came to the conclusion that she had. He also knew that, in her own words, men had been using her for their own gain for years and in her eyes, he was just another one of those, but he wasn't.

"None of that is true Jenna. I meant it when I said I love you."

"Love? You don't love anyone, but yourself. I know you're use to women falling at your feet, dropping panties as soon as you smile at them. I'm sure the woman you with the other night fell victim to your charm too."

Whoa, he thought. What woman? He cut her off before she could go any further.

"Wait Jenna. What woman? I wasn't with a woman. What night?"

His constant denial was pissing her off.

"I heard you Charles. Tuesday night. I spent the night in the apartment above my shop. Did you forget that I can hear you when I'm in the apartment above my shop and you are in yours as well, especially when there is a woman involved? I heard you. I heard the woman screaming with pleasure. I know what it's like because I've experienced it with you and a woman can't help, but scream. Let's not forget I told you about the headboard. You really need to move it off of the wall you pathetic excuse for a human being," Jenna said with so much rage, she could burst into flames at any moment. She saw the pure shock on his face when he realized he had been caught.

"I thought you were out of town Tuesday? When did you get back?" he asked.

"That's all you have to say? When did I get back? What difference does it make? I was there and I heard you and some woman going at it all night long. Well I hope she was good and I hope it was worth it to you."

She tried to pass by him. "Now get out of my way. I can't even stand looking at you right now."

He could see that she needed to get away because he could hear the change in her voice that went from anger to sorrow and hurt so he let her go without saying another word. He stood looking at her as she retreated and wondered what she was talking about. He wasn't with a woman. He thought through what she'd said. She was in town on Tuesday evening when he thought she was gone out of town to visit her friend. He knew he hadn't spent any nights at the restaurant because....AH HA!!! That's it he thought. Tuesday he had let one of his waiters, Nathan, use the apartment upstairs.

Nathan, who he had hired as a favor to Brad, had mentioned to him that he and his wife could use a night alone because they were living at his parent's house until they could save up enough money for an apartment. Nathan's wife Tammy and Cecily were best friends and Nathan had needed the job while he finished culinary school.

They had also recently had twins, which was unexpected and they were having difficulties in their relationship due to the butting in of his parents all the time. Charles offered to let him and his wife have some alone time in the apartment if they could get a babysitter for the twins and as long as they were out of the apartment before the morning crew came in to prepare for the day. That is who Jenna must have heard. He really did need to move that bed away from the adjourning wall. After she told him that she could hear his amorous activities through the wall, it never dawned on him to move it because he had not been with any other women besides her so there was never anyone on the other side of the wall that could hear them. Better yet, he needed to get the bed out of the upstairs room. It appeared, that bed had just cost him the love of his life. She was so angry, he wasn't sure she'd ever give him the chance to explain.

"Charles, the ladies are ready for the main course," one of the waitresses he'd brought in to help with the bridal shower said, coming up to him.

"I put out more appetizers because you said to keep them coming throughout the shower. You coming?" she asked, taking his thoughts briefly off of Jenna and back on to the shower.

"Yes, I'm coming right in. He was overseeing the food for the shower, something he never did, but this was his best friend's fiancé and he wanted to be sure everything was perfect. He would fix things with Jenna later. He loved her and he wasn't giving up on them.

*****

Jenna tried to avoid watching Charles every time he came into the room throughout the shower. She was glad no one in the room had heard her conversation with him earlier. She would have been mortified if any of them had known what a fool she had been. He looked at her every time he'd come in. She could feel his eyes piercing right through her. If she wasn't so angry or visually picturing him with some woman a few nights ago, she would have melted with each of his stares. All it took was one look with those gorgeous eyes of his and she was like ice cream sitting on a hot car on the hottest day of the summer.

She took her attention away from noticing him and back onto the shower as Cecily began opening her bridal shower gifts. Jenna was glad she had come. Even though it appeared things were over between she and Charles, she had enjoyed getting to know Brad and Cecily. They were a perfect couple and she was happy for the love they shared. She thought that she and Charles were on that same path. For now, she smiled her way through her pain and tried her best to enjoy the shower, even while her world was crumbling.

"Cecily that is hot!" Kasey, one of the guests said, making reference to the hot pink lingerie that was in one of the gift bags.

They all laughed when Cecily pulled out the next gift. They were a set of pink, feather covered handcuffs.

"Now I may need to take these along with this hot pink lingerie with me on my honeymoon. This is right up my alley!" Cecily shouted while laughing with a sinister smile on her face.

"Girl, I have a pair of those. Used them earlier this week."

All the ladies gave catcalls when the woman named Tammy spoke.

"Tell us more Tammy," someone said and Jenna listened in as well. She and Charles had always tried to be adventurous when it came to sex and she remembered a night that involved handcuffs and the memory brought a smile to her face. Everyone's attention, including Jenna's turned to Tammy as she spoke softly not wanting the guys who were in the other room setting up the table for the dinner to hear.

"Girls, my husband and I had not had a night like that in a long time. For those who don't know we have one year old twins and they are a handful. Between them and living at Nathan's parent's house, we never get any time alone. Tuesday night was just what we needed."

Jenna heard Tuesday and realized, everyone must have been getting busy on Tuesday night. It seems it was a night for animalistic sex!

"Nathan had planned it all out. There was wine, chocolate covered strawberries, soft music and lots of lace, leather, handcuffs and a few other toys as well. We made use of all of it all night long! It was just what we needed. Come to think of it. I need to make sure I thank Charles before I leave tonight."

Jenna couldn't stop herself from speaking even if she'd tried. She heard Charles' name and her radar went up.

"Thank Charles why?" Jenna said as all eyes turned to her.

"Oh, everyone who didn't get a chance to meet Jenna. She owns the bakery next door and is currently in a hot relationship with said Charles."

"Charles is in a relationship?" another woman said. Jenna sat, looking a little uneasy that she interrupted the story, but she couldn't ignore hearing Charles' name mentioned.

"Yes, he is actually in a relationship," Cecily said.

All eyes were on her and each pair looked at her with admiration.

"You go Jenna! That one is a hard nut to crack," another woman said.

Cecily chimed in again.

"We don't mean to make you uncomfortable Jenna. It's just that Charles doesn't really commit to a relationship and we never thought the day would come when we could even say that. If he's yours, he's yours for life. You never hear Charles and the word relationship in the same sentence. He's had his share of women, not including anyone in this room, but he's never been one to commit to anyone. Brad even told me that Charles is in love with you. I'm happy for you. I bet I'll be helping to plan a shower like this for you and gifting you your own set of fur covered handcuffs before you know it."

All the ladies clapped with excitement. Jenna just smiled, not sure how to respond to that. They didn't know that her so called relationship with Charles was over mainly because he apparently wasn't the relationship type like they suspected anyway.

"Thanks ladies, but I want to hear the rest of Tammy's story. Don't you?"

Jenna wanted to take the attention off of her and back to Tammy and why she needed to thank Charles.

"You were saying you needed to thank Charles," she added.

"Oh right," Tammy said, getting back to her

story.

"It was all Charles' idea. He knew that Nathan and I have been struggling to try and find alone time since the twins and since moving in with Nathan's parents. Did you all know that there is an apartment above the restaurant?" Tammy asked.

Jenna knew very well about the apartment.

"Well, Charles hooked us up. He had the apartment decorated with soft lighting, the wine and strawberries and the music. Of course the toys and handcuffs were all Nathan's idea, adding a lot of spice to the night just like I like. Charles let Nathan and I have a night alone in the upstairs apartment and it was just what we needed to bring the fire back into our relationship."

Tammy continued on giving the ladies information on her night with her husband when Jenna tuned them out realizing it wasn't Charles who was in the apartment on Tuesday night. It was Tammy and her husband. They are who she heard on the other side of the wall having wild sex. All week she had been hurting thinking Charles had been unfaithful to her and it wasn't him at all. She had accused him and had said some pretty harsh words to him. She was so angry, she didn't even give him a chance to really explain. She felt awful. She felt a new low when he entered the room to inform the ladies that the food was set up whenever they were ready to eat. When he did, Tammy excitedly thanked him for letting she and her husband have the night they needed in the upstairs apartment since he knew they couldn't afford a night away or in an expensive Chicago hotel.

Jenna tried to look away when he looked over at her letting her know that he tried to tell her it wasn't him. Now they both knew the truth. She tried to soften her features to let him know she was sorry for her accusation. Being the gentleman, he didn't let on that anything was wrong between the two of them. He smiled at her and then told Tammy he was glad that he could help.

"Oh wait ladies," Jenna heard Tammy say.

"I haven't told you the best news. Charles is going to hire Nathan as the new manager for the restaurant here because Sean, the current manager is going to be moving to Las Vegas to run the new restaurant Charles will be opening up there. That means more money and the opportunity for Nathan and I to finally take the kids and move into our own place. This man is a saint," Tammy said, making reference to Charles.

Everyone continued to clap as Charles exited the room, but not before looking her way once more.

Jenna felt bad. She felt really bad. She knew he wasn't devious and conniving and if she had taken the time to really listen to what he had to say, she was sure now that there was a perfectly good explanation for everything that she thought he had done to her, including her accusations about her bakery. She would hang around and try to talk to him when the shower was over. She only hoped that he would give her another chance to talk. After the things she'd said, she wasn't sure he would, but all she could do was try.

*****

The shower had finally ended. Charles had a big crowd coming in for the evening and while his staff worked to prepare the restaurant, he could finally sit down and finish signing the contracts for the new restaurant he was opening in Las Vegas. This was big for him and he couldn't help, but think that though he was making achievements beyond his imagination in the restaurant business, his personal life was currently in shambles. He had also been told that he would be getting another award for Outstanding Restaurant and Outstanding Chef of the year. He would also be honored at that evening's ceremony for his community service work supporting the many fundraising events put on by local firefighters to help combat homelessness. He was proud of the work he was doing and was thankful that he was being recognized.

He was waiting to tell Jenna when she returned from her trip, knowing she would be excited for him and he wanted her on his arm that night, sharing in the event. The thought that he wouldn't be able to enjoy it because she wouldn't be with him that night didn't sit well with him. He hated seeing her hurt and she was hurt because of him. That's not something he ever wanted to do. He did want her building, but not at the expense of his relationship. She meant more to him even than his restaurant. He wished he could get her to believe that and understand he never set out to deceive her. His intentions were true and honorable from the beginning. He looked up at hearing a soft knock on his office door.

"Come in."

The woman he was just thinking of entered. He stood up when she came in and shut the door behind her.

"Hi Charles," she said softly, hoping he could tell she wasn't as angry as she had been before.

"Hi baby."

Jenna smiled. She loved when he called her that. It made her feel all gooey inside.

"You sure you still want to call me that after the things I said to you earlier?" she asked, coming further into the room to stand right in front of him.

"I wasn't the one angry, you were," Charles said, smiling, happy to see her. "You're still here."

Jenna nodded.

"Yes I'm still here. I was hoping I could apologize before I left for the things I said to you," she admitted, looking up into the eyes that she had stared into so many times while they had been making love. She loved looking at him. His eyes told her everything she needed to know about him.

If she had taken the time to look at them earlier, she would have seen that he was being genuine when he said he never set out to hurt her and that it wasn't him with some woman in the apartment earlier in the week.

Charles reached out to capture her hands in his, pulling them to his mouth as he gave the back of her hands a light kiss.

"No apology is necessary Jenna. I understand your anger, thinking I had been deceiving you all along. I know how it sounded, especially coming out of Sean's mouth. He's so dramatic with everything, but he was wrong. I spoke to him about it and he knows he owes you an apology. He also knows he only heard one part of the conversation, something he should not have been listening to, to begin with. He's sorry and so am I."

"You have nothing to apologize for Charles. I should be apologizing for being so accusatory and definitely for the way I spoke to you. I was just so angry, but I should have listened to you when you tried to explain."

"Jenna, baby, I love you and let's just put all of this mess behind us. I don't want to fight. You know that's not my best stance," he said, giving her the eye that let her know he was thinking of his better qualities, the same thing she was thinking.

Without any further words, he leaned down and planted the softest, sweetest kiss on her lips. It wasn't he who turned the kiss into something more, but it was her. His kisses were addictive and intoxicating and she would never tire of them. She wanted more so when he continued with the soft kissing, she took his mouth aggressively, slipping her tongue between his lips to capture the tongue that could do amazing things to all parts of her body. He let her take the lead and she did. She hungrily feasted on him, reaching up to grab his shoulders, trying to bring him further down towards her while leaning into him.

Charles knew when Jenna's body was in need and he could and would never deny her. He reached down and grasped her legs, drawing her skirt further up her legs. When he had it up around her waist, he pulled her legs up until they locked behind his back. They continued kissing like their lives depended on it while he walked backwards with her in his arms toward the door to be sure it was locked. He wanted no interruptions. When he was sure it was locked, he turned back around and placed her on the top of his desk, thankful for the soft, leather padding that covered the edges of his desk. He was about to take her hard and fast and he didn't want her getting any splinters in that perfect round behind he loved so much.

Jenna's level of excitement went sky high. She had missed Charles all week. She had missed this all week. She loved that he was always ready for pleasure no matter where they were. The excitement was making her toes curl, even in her five inch Maddens.

"I've missed you," Jenna said softly in his ears right before slipping her tongue into it, something she knew he loved. His moan after her entry into his ear let her know that he had missed her just as much.

"I've missed you too baby, more than you can begin to imagine." He continued to speak while reaching under down to remove her silken thong from her body, sliding them slowly down her legs.

"I knew you were angry with me, but still I wanted you here with me."

"I don't ever want to be apart from you again. I love you. I love you so much," Jenna said with a voice laden with love and a lot of lust and desire for him. She wanted him to hurry up and stop prolonging giving her what she had been missing all week.

"Can you stop with the slowness now? I need you," she said, almost not being able to wait. She quickly reached for his belt, almost ripping it off before fumbling with his zipper. It wouldn't have been so complicated if he had not been so aroused. His erection was putting a strain on the zipper and she needed to be careful when unzipping them so that she didn't injure a part of him that she loved so very much.

Charles could tell Jenna was struggling trying to get his pants down so as soon as he was able to get her blouse open enough to pull her breasts out of the bright blue bra that was straining to contain the huge globes he loved caressing, sucking and loving on, he reached down to help her remove enough of his clothes so that they could both get the relief they needed. They also needed to this connection again. They had been apart for almost a week and that was the longest they had gone without him being in her body since they'd met and he needed her badly. The way he noticed her hands shaking as she helped divest him of his clothes, he knew she needed him just as much.

When he was able to slide his pants and his boxers down his legs, Jenna reached out to caress just the tip of his jutting manhood and when she did, Charles through his head back, enjoying the feel of her once again. As she started rubbing the early essence of his excitement for her around the head, he reached out to halt her actions. He had missed her so much, just the mere delight of being this close to her again would put an end to this adventure, much sooner than he wanted. Charles grasped her hands and placed them around his neck as he moved closer into the cradle of her legs.

They were both breathing heavily and anxiously as he grabbed her behind, moving her closer to the edge so that he could slide right into her until he was buried so far, they could barely tell where she began and he ended. Being inside of her again like this was like new money. He didn't wait to give them what they both desired. After plunging in, he retreated until he was almost out of her body before heading back in with ferocity. He was being aggressive in his lovemaking and he loved that Jenna was along for the ride, back where he wanted her to be. She was matching him plunge for plunge, over and over they rode each other until together they crested. Charles saw stars as he closed his eyes reveling in the feel of Jenna's body as it gripped him in a vice hold, a hold that he couldn't wait to experience for the rest of his life with her.

Jenna kept her legs wrapped around Charles' back even after they were both too exhausted to even speak. She didn't want to release him from her body just yet. She had missed this feeling. She had missed the closeness and she would never, ever be without it again.

"I love you Charles. You are my world baby," she said as she leaned back onto the desk, pulling him down with her, caressing him by rubbing her hands up and down his muscular back. She was too exhausted to continue sitting straight up.

"I love you too Jenna. Forever and always. Should I wait until we're dressed and not in this current position before I ask you to marry me?" he said, clearly shocking her as her hands stopped moving on his back. He hoped it was a good shock because he couldn't imagine his life without her. He continued laying on her chest waiting for some type of response. When none came, he leaned up on his arms to look down at her and what he saw was tears streaming down her cheeks onto his desk. He reached up to wipe them away, but she stopped him.

"No don't. You never wipe away tears of joy. I'm crying because I want nothing more than to be your wife whether you ask me when we are naked or fully clothed. The answer would be the same. Yes! I will marry you, anytime, anywhere. I love..."

The rest of her words were smothered as Charles kissed her, showing her how much he loved her and wanted to thank her for giving him a chance to love her like she should be loved. A love that only he could give her. While he continued kissing her, he reached over, sliding the top drawer of his desk open and retrieved a small velvet ring box. When he had it in his hand, he broke off the kiss, not really wanting to, but he wanted to make the moment very special by giving her the ring he had purchased over a week ago, when he'd first wanted to propose to her.

Jenna saw the box in his hand and with a lot of excitement, she thrust her hand out to him wiggling her fingers, encouraging him to place the ring that she knew had to be in the box on her finger.

"I want you to open the box, not me," he said, loving her extra, jubilant response at seeing the ring box.

She looked into his eyes before taking the box in her hands and opening it to see the most magnificent ring she'd ever seen in her life. It was so perfect for her. Not just because of the size or the way it sparkled, but because it came from the man who had quickly stolen her heart and she was glad he held it.

"Jenna Taylor, will you marry me and make my life complete?"

"Yes Charles. I will marry you."

Jenna looked from him to the ring.

"I love it. It's so beautiful."

"So are you baby, so are you," he replied.

He wasted no time taking the ring out of the box and placing it on her finger. It was a perfect fit thanks to a little snooping into her jewelry box he had done one night at her house. He had measured a ring he knew she often wore so that he could tell his jeweler her size.

"You make me so happy," Jenna said on a moan when she realized Charles had started moving in and out of her body again, already once again painfully hard and stiff inside of her.

Charles didn't speak. He simply groaned out his acknowledgement of her comment, about to take them both on another ride. Jenna reached up to encase his neck with her arms again while locking her legs tighter around his back ready to go higher and higher with him again. She realized she was right where she wanted and needed to be.

EPILOGUE

One month later

"Our next award recipient has not only been recognized tonight for having this year's outstanding restaurant of the year, along with Chef of the year, but he is also being honored for his work in the community. This year, he didn't hesitate to not only write an enormous check to help the firefighters cause to provide food, blankets and clothing for local shelters helping the homeless, but he cooks and provides meals once a week to three of the shelters right here in Chicago along with serving at one every Monday afternoon. It is with great pleasure that I present an additional award for public service to Master Chef Charles Watts."

The room went crazy with applause and Jenna could see that it was a standing ovation. She was so proud of Charles and all that he had accomplished. She was especially proud of the work he did in the community. She leaned up and gave him the kiss he reached down for, before heading towards the stage to accept his award. He was so handsome in his all black tuxedo and white shirt with a touch of a red handkerchief in his breast pocket that matched the red gown she had chosen to wear for the evening.

"Thank you for this honor. I have a few people I'd like to thank tonight. First I give thanks to the Almighty, for making everything possible. I'd also like to thank my staff for always providing five star service at the restaurant and most of them help each week with the shelters. They don't have to do that, but I'm glad they see the need without me having to ask them.

I want to thank my family and friends who are here tonight to celebrate with me. Some of my family came as far away as Seattle for this and I want them to know I appreciate their love and support.

I also want to thank the society for the honor tonight. I do what I do because I love this great city of Chicago. Sometimes I wonder if I'm doing anything besides providing a great place for people to come and eat. It's a pleasure knowing that I can help the community who can't afford to eat at my restaurant, but who also deserve having at least three meals a day. I'm thankful for being able to provide that," Charles said.

The room broke out into even more applause as he continued on, not forgetting the most important thank you of the evening.

"Now, I can't sit down until I thank the most important person here tonight. My fiancé Jenna Taylor. Yes, the love of my life agreed to be my wife one month ago tonight. I am a better man because of her. I won't go into how we met, but I will say it was the best day of my life. I have an announcement to make, if that's okay," he said, addressing his comments to the host for the night. Seeing the acknowledgement that it was okay, he turned back to the microphone and looked into the eyes of the woman who made his life complete.

"Jenna took over her father's bakery after his passing, wanting to keep his dream alive. She did so even when she had dreams of her own to open a center to offer after school tutoring and other fun activities for kids to have someplace safe to hang out. That shows what a caring and loving person she is and I love her deeply for that."

Charles could tell his ever emotional soon to be wife, was about to cry. He could see the unshed tears in her eyes, overwhelmed that he was taking a night that was about him and placing the spotlight on her. That was just the kind of humbled person she was. He turned to signal for a few of his friends who were carrying a covered board to bring it up on the stage. Everyone in the room stood to get a better look at what was going on.

"Jenna, can you please come up on the stage?" Charles asked.

He watched as Brad escorted Jenna from her seat

to the stage.

"Ladies and gentleman, in further support of not only this community, but in support of Jenna's desire to make a difference, I bring you the Aaron Taylor Recreation and Community Center."

Jenna's heart stopped when the men unveiled what was behind the cloth. It showed the design of a gigantic center, named after her father, Aaron Taylor.

She finally did cry then. She continued to cry, trying to see the plans through her tears as Charles continued to talk.

"Recently Jenna and I had talked about plans to move her bakery to a different location that would enable her to expand her business. That was all fine until I realized I wanted her to not only continue her father's dream of keeping the bakery open, but to also live her dream as well. Instead of moving the bakery, we're going to expand the restaurant not only out, but up to add in a level that will house the bakery right above the restaurant. As a pre-wedding gift, we will be using what was going to be the new bakery location and building the community center which will have several class rooms for tutoring and learning as well as a swimming pool, outdoor basketball court, indoor gym, a full kitchen, a theater and plenty of space to one day add in a full daycare center, offering free daycare to young mothers who are still high school aged so that they don't feel like they have to drop out of school, but can further their education knowing their children will be taken care of during the day. The center won't be advocating teen pregnancy, but will offer classes on prevention as well as having full time counselors on staff."

He turned back to Jenna. "I love you baby," he said to her right before she threw herself into his arms, crying out her thank you for being the most wonderful man she'd ever known, besides her father.

"I love you," she was able to get out in between sniffles. Others came towards the stage to also get a closer look as the applause and cheers in the room continued on and on.

"Thank you," Charles said before escorting Jenna off the stage so that she could gather herself. Before he could get far the host for the evening cleared his throat in the microphone, getting everyone's attention.

"Charles, this is an incredible thing you and Jenna will be doing for the community. The society would like to partner with you on this and make a donation of one million dollars to help with the center."

The crowd went wild. Charles was stunned. He wasn't expecting that. He mouthed a thank you to everyone at the generosity of the society that had honored him tonight. He was even more elated when several others in the crowd also pledged financial support. He noticed in a group that was clearly not ready to sit and stop cheering that others were approaching the stage and bringing check after check in support of the center. It was important to make your mark in the world, not just in the business you did, but in the way of support you lend to the community that surrounds you.

*****

Later that evening, Jenna waited in bed for Charles to finish making sure the house was all locked up and secure. She looked around and never in her wildest dreams did she ever think that she would be this happy.

"Thinking about me?" Charles said as he entered the bedroom and noticed the smile on Jenna's face.

"Always."

"That's good. That's how I want it to be always," he said, joining her in bed.

"Tonight was incredible Charles. I was sitting here reading over the entire proposal and this is more than I could have ever dreamed of."

"I'm glad baby. I want to fulfill all of your dreams if I can. It makes me happy to know you're happy. With the additional donations we received tonight and from others that are pouring in, we'll actually be able to hire all of the full-time staff you'll need and the daycare can open up at the same time that the center will be opening. It's in a separate building and we were initially going to have to wait before adding that on, but the millions of dollars that we received in donations tonight will leave us with a big surplus even after all of the construction. Most of those who donated tonight even committed to yearly donations to help keep the center up and running. It was your idea that started all of this," he said with appreciation.

Jenna turned to look at him.

"When did you have time to do all of this?"

"A little while ago, before that one day when you were angry with me. I wasn't sure if it could be done, but I had my people working in the background and it all turned out great. I was planning to share it with you but I didn't want to get your hopes up high if things did work out," he said, pulling her into his arms

"You are my hero, my everything, my all I could ever ask for. You know that right?" she said, looking at him with all the love she could muster up.

"I plan to be that for the rest of our lives. Speaking of, have you decided on a date for the wedding yet? All this shacking up is great, but I'm ready to change that last name of yours," Charles said, snuggling in closer.

"I'm thinking June," she said.

"June? That's months away. I don't want to wait that long," he said while planting small kissing along the column of Jenna's neck.

She was finding it hard to concentrate when Charles' kisses were joined by caresses.

"Okay, then what about April then," she replied,

barely able to get the words out because her body had taken over all of her thinking for her.

"November," Charles offered.

"November? That's in two months. I can't plan a wedding in two months. What about February, around Valentine's day," she counteroffered, about to lose all sense of speech because Charles had now untied the strings that held her nightie together across her breasts and had snaked his tongue inside. Jenna was losing all focus now.

"November," was all Charles replied, not budging.

"Baby, okay, January is my final offer," she said, helping him to fully remove her nightie from her body.

Charles pulled her body so that she was now under him after removing her clothing. He didn't have to worry about removing anything. He had never put anything on after his shower. He looked into her eyes right before taking her lips in a kiss that held promise for the rest of the night.

"November, baby," he said, coming up for air.

At this point, Jenna could feel what was waiting for her, lying hard and heavy on top of her and she couldn't resist anymore.

"November," she whispered before all talking stopped and thoughts of anything, including the wedding disappeared from her mind as it filled with the pleasure that she was about to receive. Right now, she would give him anything he asked for.

Go back to the beginning and get your copy of the 1ˢᵗ first book in the Amorous Occupations series, The Artist, now available in paperwork and e-Pub.

THE ARTIST

Zora Michaels, a local Boston artist spends all of her time working and focused on her next achievement. The war in Iraq took the life of the one man who loved her and her bohemian, artsy lifestyle. She no longer wants love. She only wants to paint. Micah Prentiss had the perfect life, a beautiful wife, a baby about to come into the world, when that world changed with her sudden passing during child-birth. The only love he ever wanted to experience again was the love he had for his child until the passion he found in a painting reminded him of what true love is all about. Come discover a second chance at love that will last forever!!

Get your copy of 2nd book in the Amorous Occupations series, The Bookkeeper, now available in paperback and e-Pub.

THE BOOKKEEPER

FBI agent Karen Jacobs is finally getting her first undercover assignment. Her cover assignment as a bookkeeper is an easy transition for her with her background in finance. Business owner Thomas Atwater couldn't believe his eyes when he saw the love of his life walk into the restaurant where he was having lunch. Seeing her sparked feelings he thought had died long ago when she walked out on him. Karen, discovering the object of the investigation is Thomas, the one and only man she ever truly loved, has to find a way to do her job while fighting feelings for him that she thought she had buried years ago.

Join Author Cheryl Barton for her next installment in the Amorous Occupations series with the release of the 4th book, "The Dancer" scheduled for release in mid-November 2013.

Other romance novels available by
Author *Cheryl Barton*:

Bachelor Not For Sale
Duron & Taija's story

A Designed Affair
Loren & Mike's story

Available November 2013
Perfect Combination
Tyrone & Victoria's story

All books are available on Amazon.com

Looking to publish your own novel?
Contact Barton Book Publishing at
www.bartonbookpublishing.net, where
Your Dreams Are Safe in Our Hands!

Barton Book Publishing
P.O. Box 962
Reisterstown, Maryland 21136
410-921-9417
Email: Consult@bartonbookpublishing.net

ABOUT THE AUTHOR

Cheryl Barton lives in Maryland and in her spare time she enjoys reading, writing, spending time with her family, line dancing and eating Maryland steamed crabs.

Visit her website at http://www.cherylbarton.net and be sure to leave her a comment. You can connect with her on Twitter @mscbarton and on Facebook at Author Cheryl Barton.

www.ingramcontent.com/pod-product-compliance
Lightning Source LLC
Chambersburg PA
CBHW052145170626
46812CB00004B/1602